HOMECOMING TALES

15 INSPIRING STORIES FROM OLD FRIENDS SENIOR DOG SANCTUARY

OLD FRIENDS SENIOR DOG SANCTUARY

WRITTEN BY TAMA FORTNER

Homecoming Tales: 15 Inspiring Stories from Old Friends Senior Dog Sanctuary

Tommy Nelson, PO Box 141000, Nashville, TN 37214

Published in Nashville, Tennessee, by Tommy Nelson. Tommy Nelson is an imprint of Thomas Nelson. Thomas Nelson is a registered trademark of HarperCollins Christian Publishing, Inc.

The writer is represented by Cyle Young of C.Y.L.E. (Cyle Young Literary Elite, LLC), a literary agency.

Tommy Nelson titles may be purchased in bulk for educational, business, fundraising, or sales promotional use. For information, please e-mail SpecialMarkets@ThomasNelson.com.

Written by Tama Fortner
Illustrated by Rotem Teplow
Cover photo by Mandy Whitley Photography

ISBN 978-1-4002-2293-3 (audiobook)
ISBN 978-1-4002-2291-9 (eBook)

Library of Congress Cataloging-in-Publication Data

Names: Fortner, Tama, 1969- author.
Title: Homecoming tales : 15 inspiring stories from Old Friends Senior Dog Sanctuary / written by Tama Fortner.
Description: Nashville, TN : Thomas Nelson, 2020. | Includes bibliographical references. | Audience: Ages 8-12 | Summary: "With stories of inspiration and adventure, doggy profiles and fun facts, sweet tales of older dogs' adventures, a full-color photo insert, and plenty of canine kisses, Homecoming Tales is sure to follow your young reader home"-- Provided by publisher.
Identifiers: LCCN 2020021810 (print) | LCCN 2020021811 (ebook) | ISBN 9781400222926 (paperback) | ISBN 9781400222919 (epub)
Subjects: LCSH: Animal sanctuaries--Tennessee--Anecdotes. | Dog rescue--Tennessee--Anecdotes.
Classification: LCC HV4746 .F67 2020 (print) | LCC HV4746 (ebook) | DDC 636.7/08320976854--dc23
LC record available at https://lccn.loc.gov/2020021810
LC ebook record available at https://lccn.loc.gov/2020021811

Printed in the United States

20 21 22 23 24 LSCC 10 9 8 7 6 5 4 3 2 1

Mfr: LSCC / Crawfordsville, IN / October 2020 / PO #9589867

CONTENTS

OLD FRIENDS SENIOR DOG SANCTUARY

Step inside the Old Friends Senior Dog Sanctuary, and you'll meet all kinds of new old friends!

Shelby is out playing with the big dogs. Shelby is a lively husky mix with the prettiest eyes you've ever seen—one bright blue and one golden brown. Miles is probably napping in his favorite spot right outside the laundry room door. Miles could barely walk when he first arrived at Old Friends. But with a little medicine and a lot of love, this chocolate-colored Lab mix is now up and moving—when he's not napping. And then there's Tank. At 120 pounds, this gray giant definitely lives up to his name! Don't let his size fool you though. Tank is pure sweetness and is just looking for a family to love.

These three are just some of the wonderful and amazing dogs at Old Friends. Sure, they're a little older than the average doggo, but each of them needs the love, care, and safety of a forever home. Many people who want to adopt a dog walk right past these sweet seniors. But not Michael and Zina Goodin.

Years ago the Goodins began to notice all the older dogs in need of homes, and they began to dream. One day there would be a place for these dogs. One day older dogs would have all the vet care they needed. And one day the Goodins would create a program so that senior dogs would always have a home.

That one day came in 2012 in a little city called Mt. Juliet, just outside of Nashville, Tennessee. Zina and Michael opened a home for older dogs and called it Old Friends Senior Dog Sanctuary.

It All Started with a Dream

The dream for Old Friends began when Zina and Michael were working with Middle Tennessee Golden Retriever

Rescue. Because of their sweet personalities and beautiful smiles, golden retrievers (or goldens) are one of the most popular of all dog breeds. Yet most people coming to the rescue to adopt a dog wanted puppies or younger dogs. The older goldens were being passed by.

Michael and Zina realized that if the goldens weren't getting adopted, then it must be much worse for dogs of less popular breeds. Those dogs weren't even making it out of the animal control shelters. You see, each year, over three million dogs end up in shelters. While many are adopted, many are not. Over 670,000 shelter dogs are **euthanized**, or put to sleep, every year. It's done by giving them a shot that stops the brain, heart, and lungs from working. It's quick and painless, and it isn't done because the shelters don't care. They simply don't have the money or the space to keep all of the dogs. They have to focus on the animals that have the best chance of being adopted. Dogs who are older or injured or have medical needs are most in danger of being put to sleep.

Michael and Zina saw this happening and decided to do their part to help. Over the next couple years, whenever a senior dog arrived at the rescue, Zina and Michael took it home. At one point, they had eight beautiful golden retrievers and golden mixes living with them. Just imagine! That's eight smiling golden faces to say hello to you every morning, eight wagging tails, eight wiggly balls of golden goodness to hug, and eight ready-to-play partners for a game of fetch.

Then along came Lucy-Lu. This sweet golden overcame a terrible, terrible past and went on to live a rich, full, and happy life with Michael and Zina. From the moment she arrived at their house, Lucy-Lu was smiling. And she never stopped smiling the whole time she lived with the Goodins. Lucy-Lu's joy proved to the Goodins that they could make a real difference in the lives of older dogs. And she inspired them to find a way to bring that same joy to the lives of other senior dogs. Michael and Zina will tell you that in her own way, Lucy-Lu was one of the cofounders of Old Friends.

The Old Friends Senior Dog Sanctuary officially began in April 2012 in Michael and Zina's home. With plenty of fences, gates, and room to roam—as well as plenty of cozy dog beds inside the house—Michael and Zina provided a safe place, or **sanctuary**, for a number of dogs. When they needed more space, the Goodins purchased a cabin and land next door. But with so many dogs in need of rescue, they quickly outgrew that space as well.

GrandPaw's Gardens

In 2017 Old Friends purchased an old garden center in Mt. Juliet, Tennessee. Inside the building, they created spaces for all of the dogs—no dog would ever have to live outside in the rain or cold again. Comfy couches, cozy cubbies, and dog beds of all shapes and sizes filled every possible spot. The Goodins and their staff carved out a kitchen and a laundry area. They even made a place for a small examining room for the vet. Outside the building, they added gates and fences for play areas, one for the bigger dogs as well as one for the smaller guys. And then, to make the transformation complete, they changed the name to "GrandPaw's Gardens."

A Day in the Life of an Old Friend

These dogs may be seniors, but their days are full of fun.

7:00 a.m. to 8:00 a.m.: rise and shine
9:00 a.m.: breakfast and outside business
playtime
12:00 p.m.: nap time
playtime
5:00 p.m.: dinnertime and outside business
playtime
8:00 p.m.: good night, old friends!

To rest up from all this eating and playing, couches, chairs, and dog beds are scattered everywhere throughout the sanctuary—perfect for taking a break from all the action.

Now roughly eighty-five to one hundred dogs at a time make their home at GrandPaw's Gardens, with hundreds more in foster homes. A full-time **veterinarian**—Dr. Christine—makes sure the dogs get all the care, medications, and treatments they need. The organization that began with just Michael, Zina, Lucy-Lu, and a dream now has over thirty employees and more than seventy volunteers. Since their beginning in 2012, Old Friends has helped more than one thousand senior dogs find the loving homes they need.

Finding Old Friends

In the beginning of Old Friends, Michael and Zina visited area shelters to find old dogs in need of rescue. Occasionally they would take in a stray dog. But these days, Old Friends only takes dogs from shelters. That's because these dogs are the most in danger of being put to sleep. In fact, the shelters now call Michael and Zina when a senior dog comes in. Old Friends works directly with about five to six different local shelters to rescue dogs.

Old Friends tries to only take dogs that are ten years or older—true senior dogs. However, it can be hard to tell exactly how old a dog is, especially if it is sick or dirty. Once, Michael and Zina thought they were picking up a fourteen-year-old male dog from a shelter. When their vet examined the dog, they learned "he" was a "she." And *she* was a six-month-old puppy. A terrible case of **mange** (a skin disease) made her look and act much older. Even though she was a puppy, Old Friends healed her and found her a home.

Old Friends will take as many dogs as they can, as long as they have room—or a forever foster willing to take a dog. Sometimes that means they have more smaller dogs than larger ones, simply because the smaller dogs take up less space.

Because they keep their dogs together in groups, Old Friends can't take dogs that fight other dogs. And because there are so many people in and out of the sanctuary, they also can't take dogs that bite people. So what happens if they find out a dog bites or doesn't get along with other dogs *after* it comes to the sanctuary? *That dog stays.* They make special arrangements for it. No dog who comes to Old Friends *ever* goes back to a shelter.

Welcome, Doggos!

Once a dog is picked up from a shelter, it first gets checked out by the vet. The dog will get any treatments, vaccines, or medicines it needs. Then the dog goes into **quarantine** in the vet's office. That means it stays by itself to make sure it doesn't have any sicknesses that might spread to the other dogs.

Next, the dog will walk around on a leash with an Old Friends worker for a few days. This lets the dog get used to the sanctuary. It also allows the worker to learn the dog's personality. Smaller dogs will then head over to the Land of the Littles. Bigger dogs move out to the Garden Gang, where they can come and go through their own giant doggy door as often as they please.

In the front office area where the workers are, you'll also find quite a few dogs roaming around. These are the dogs who need a little extra attention, such as those who are blind or deaf or handicapped in some other way.

Except for a very few dogs who need special care, all of the dogs—from the Land of the Littles to the Garden Gang—are waiting for someone to come and take them home.

What Are Forever Fosters?

Old Friends is different from most other rescue shelters. Their dogs are not up for adoption. Instead, people who want to welcome an old friend into their home become a **forever foster**. What's the difference? In an adoption, the dog legally belongs to its new family. Dogs fostered through Old Friends still belong to the sanctuary. That means that if a foster can't keep a dog—if the person gets sick or something else happens in their life—that dog

never, ever goes back to a shelter. It *always* has a home at Old Friends.

Foster dogs from Old Friends also always have free vet care at the sanctuary. Zina and Michael realized that the reason many people weren't adopting senior dogs was that they were afraid the dogs would need expensive medical care. Old Friends has their own vet on staff, so they are able to take care of all the vet bills and medications. Because the dogs must come to Old Friends for vet care, forever fosters need to live within a hundred miles of the sanctuary.

If someone falls in love with one of the dogs on social media, they must apply to be a foster. They can't just come and pick up the dog. Old Friends' foster process makes sure its dogs go to loving homes. To become a forever foster, a person must first fill out a form to answer questions about their family, their home, and other pets. Next, someone from Old Friends will come to inspect their home and make sure it's a good, safe place for a dog. Old Friends also wants their dogs to be a part of the family, which means they must live inside the house. No doghouses for these pups!

Old Friends now has more than 400 dogs placed in over 250 different forever foster families. You can find out more about the forever foster program—and how to become one—on their website at www.ofsds.org. If you don't live near the sanctuary, check with rescues and shelters near you for senior dogs looking for a forever home.

Come and Get It!

Feeding time happens twice a day at Old Friends. It's a huge—and noisy—job! Because even though these guys can't read a clock, they somehow know exactly when it's time to eat. Just imagine the barking, yipping, and howling of about a hundred doggos all telling you how hungry they are! But you can't simply pour out a big bag of food and let everyone dive in. No, these sweet seniors have *lots* of different needs, so there are *many* different kinds of food. Many of the dogs also need medicine mixed into their food. In fact, almost every old friend has a little something different in its dish.

Auntie Stew

Auntie Stew is an Old Friends original recipe. Michael and Zina worked with a vet to create this super-healthy, super-yummy treat. To make Auntie Stew, Julie packs meats, vegetables, and fruits into a gigantic twenty-two-quart Crock-Pot. (That's big enough to hold five and a half gallons of milk.) The stew cooks all day until it becomes a mush that looks a lot like canned pumpkin. Each dog gets a spoonful on top of its kibble. Old Friends cooks up about ten gallons of Auntie Stew every week. If you'd like to make your own Auntie Stew for your four-legged friend, you'll find the recipe in the back of this book.

With all the foods and medicines, it's no surprise that Old Friends' kitchen is a bit like a mad scientist's laboratory. Dozens of different boxes, bags, and bins are filled with different kinds of foods. There's wet food and dry food, soft food and crunchy food. Baskets holding all the different medicines are stacked high on the shelves. But don't worry! Julie is the whiz who runs the kitchen. She's an expert at knowing exactly where everything is and which dog needs which food and what kind of medicine. A huge chart on the wall lists every single dog and helps Julie and the rest of the kitchen staff get just the right stuff into each bowl.

To get ready for the breakfast rush, one of the kitchen workers comes in at six in the morning and prepares the food. Other workers come in a little later. Before breakfast they put each dog in its own crate so no one can sneak bites from another dog's bowl. Each dog has its own bowl with its name on it. The bowls are filled and then loaded onto carts and wheeled out to the dogs. Once all the dogs are fed, workers put away the crates and collect the bowls. From start to finish, breakfast takes two to three hours. Then they do it all over again at dinnertime.

To keep everything fresh and clean, every bowl is washed after every meal. And at GrandPaw's Gardens, there's no dishwasher. Imagine washing one hundred dog bowls by hand—twice a day, every day!

mlem: the sound a dog makes when it licks something—usually something yummy, like Auntie Stew!

Wash, Dry, Fold, Repeat . . . *and* Repeat, *and* Repeat

When you have eighty-five to one hundred dogs roaming around, that also means there are eighty-five to one hundred beds and blankets for those dogs. And those beds and blankets get dirty—*fast*! Laundry is a major job at Old Friends, and volunteers take care of every bit of it. They wash, dry, and fold about twelve hundred pounds of laundry a day.

In the early days of the sanctuary, volunteers had only a regular-size washer and dryer—just like the ones you probably have at home. They also carried bags and bags *and bags* of laundry to a Laundromat to wash. Now they are so grateful to have an industrial-size washer and dryer. The washer can do eighty pounds of laundry in thirty minutes. The dryer—which heats up to two hundred degrees Fahrenheit—will dry a hundred pounds of wet laundry in just thirty minutes. Even with those huge machines, volunteers keep the

laundry moving from eight in the morning until eight at night.

When everything's clean, all the blankets need to be folded and put away. Bedcovers need to be matched to their beds and zipped back on. Because there are dozens of different shapes and sizes of dogs, there are dozens of different sizes and shapes of beds. Putting them all back together is like playing a giant matching game!

Social Media Has Gone to the Dogs!

You may have heard people talking about how social media can be a bad thing. Well, it has really gone to the dogs—and that's actually a *great* thing! Old Friends Senior Dog Sanctuary keeps its followers up-to-date with pictures and stories of its four-legged friends on Facebook and Instagram. And these senior superstars have developed quite the following. About two *million* people follow their adorable pictures! Superstars like Mack, Bella, Cash, and Tank get likes, shares, and comments from all over the world, including Australia, Ireland, and Japan.

People also come from all over the world to tour the Old Friends Senior Dog Sanctuary and meet all of their favorite social media stars.

You Can Help Old Friends Too

The sanctuary does so much for the dogs in its care—from giving them a safe home and just the right food to making sure they get all the vet care and medicines they need. As you can probably imagine though, all that care can get pretty expensive.

Most of Old Friends' money comes from donations. While some of those donations come through Facebook fundraisers and special giving holidays like Giving Tuesday, most come from ordinary people just like you. And most donations are less than twenty-five dollars. *You* can raise twenty-five dollars! Here are some ideas of how you can raise money to help Old Friends help senior dogs:

- Ask for donations instead of gifts on your birthday.
- Have a bake sale.
- Collect your family's spare change in a jar.
- Have a yard sale.
- Hold a car wash.
- Babysit, mow lawns, or rake leaves.

Bigger and Better Is on the Way

While GrandPaw's Gardens has been a big blessing for Old Friends and hundreds of senior dogs, the sanctuary

is once again outgrowing its building. In January 2020, they broke ground on a brand-new building. Designed just for Old Friends, it will have everything needed to take the best possible care of the dogs. The building itself will be almost three times bigger than the building at GrandPaw's Gardens. And instead of just two and a half acres of land, the new site will have over nine and a half acres of land—that's bigger than *seven* football fields! The dogs will have plenty of room to run and play and roam. There will even be wooded trails for nice, long walks with their people pals.

Fun Fact

Old Friends' dogs step out into the community through visits to nursing homes and assisted-living centers, as well as local pet adoption days. These snappy seniors host craft fairs and meet and greets. They even had their own party to watch the eclipse back in 2018.

The new building will also have a full-size industrial kitchen complete with a dishwasher. No more hand washing all those bowls! An air-conditioned laundry will also make life much easier for the volunteers. And Dr. Christine is thrilled to be getting a full veterinary clinic, where she'll be able to do everything from X-rays to surgeries.

Still Wagging

When you walk into Old Friends, one of the first things you might notice is how many *different* dogs there are—big dogs and little dogs, friendly dogs and shy dogs. And they come from all kinds of different backgrounds. Some were strays living on the streets. Some were rescued from horrible situations. Some were abandoned, and others were simply orphaned when their owners passed away.

"One of the most amazing things," Michael says, "is how well all these dogs get along. Some of them come from great backgrounds; some come from not-so-great backgrounds. But they get along. Oh sure, we will have a spat once in a while. But for the most part, they all come in and they make buddies here."

These dogs don't care about spotted coats or fancy collars. They understand that coming from different backgrounds doesn't mean they can't be pals. All these dogs want to know is whether their fellow dogs (or people) are up for a good game of tug-of-war or a nice, long stroll through GrandPaw's Gardens.

At Old Friends Senior Dog Sanctuary, dogs that were thrown away, left behind, or forgotten find a home. Love and care—and a good game of fetch—are the rules of the

day. As Zina says, "There's nothing we can do about their pasts, so we have to make their life as good as possible while we have them."

That's why the people at Old Friends work hard to make sure each dog has plenty of reasons to wag its tail every day.

LUCY-LU AND LEO

THE INSPIRATION AND THE ROCK STAR

Before Michael and Zina opened the sanctuary, they owned two extra-special senior dogs. One was Lucy-Lu, a beautiful golden retriever. She overcame a horrible past and inspired the dream that turned into Old Friends Senior Dog Sanctuary. The other dog was Leo, who was big, fuzzy, and full of personality. Known to his adoring fans as Leo the Lion and Leo the Rock Star, his gorgeous mane captured hearts the world over. After his rescue, Leo quickly became the puppy-eyed face of Old Friends. Together, these two seniors' second-chance stories led to the rescue of hundreds of other dogs.

Meet Lucy-Lu

BREED: golden retriever

AGE: 14

SIZE: 70 pounds

GENDER: female

LUCY-LU'S PEOPLE: Zina and Michael Goodin

FUN FACT

Lucy-Lu *loved* the snow and rain. Every time snowflakes or raindrops started to fall, you'd find her outside. Her most favorite thing to do was make snow angels—she would lie on her back and wiggle and squirm for as long as the snow lasted. When it rained, off she'd go, running through the raindrops, getting soaked, and splashing through the mud.

Rescued from the Dark

The basement was dark, and the smell was terrible. Lucy-Lu huddled in her too-small cage. It was so tiny, she couldn't even stand up or stretch out. Her tummy ached with hunger. It had been days, maybe even weeks, since she had eaten. Stacked high all around her were other cages filled with other hungry, hurting dogs.

Lucy-Lu was part of a **puppy mill**. Her owner kept Lucy-Lu and dozens of other dogs in wire cages and used them to breed puppies to sell. That was terrible enough, but then the owner decided she didn't want to breed the dogs anymore. Instead of taking care of the dogs or finding new homes for them, she left them in their cages and closed the basement door.

Thankfully, something went wrong inside the house and a repairman was called. He saw the dogs and reported the owner for her cruelty and neglect.

One day, light poured into the basement and a soft voice spoke to Lucy-Lu. Gentle hands unlocked the cage, lifted her out, and carried her into the sunshine. That day, twenty-five golden retrievers were saved, along with dozens of other dogs of several different breeds.

Lucy-Lu was about ten years old when she was rescued from that basement. No one knows how long she had lived there. When she was rescued, she weighed only about thirty pounds—*half* what a healthy female golden should weigh. She was too weak to walk, and you could count each of her ribs. Lucy-Lu almost didn't make it.

She was taken in by Middle Tennessee Golden Retriever Rescue—the group that Zina and Michael were working

with at that time. The Goodins already had one senior dog in their fur-family, and they knew they wanted to adopt another. When Lucy-Lu arrived at the rescue, Michael and Zina agreed to take her home.

But first, Lucy-Lu had to recover. She spent a month getting medical care to restore her health, along with special foods to help her get back to a healthy weight. At last, when she was strong enough, Michael and Zina picked her up and took her home.

PUPPY MILLS

A puppy mill is a place where dogs are bred under cruel and unhealthy conditions in order to get large numbers of puppies to sell. According to the Humane Society, there are over ten thousand puppy mills in the United States. Each year they produce about two million puppies. These puppies are often sold in pet stores or online. Puppy mills care little for the parent dogs, keeping them locked in cages their entire lives.

If you're buying a puppy, remember that a good breeder will be happy to show you where their puppies are born and will allow you to meet the adult dogs. And of course, there are so many dogs—of all ages—just waiting to be adopted in rescues and shelters all across the country.

Ready to Run!

The Goodins will never forget that first day Lucy-Lu came home. "She jumped out of the car, and she hit the yard smiling," Zina says. "She just left the past behind and kept going. She smiled the whole time she was with us. She never let anything get her down."

After years spent living in a tiny cage, Lucy-Lu was definitely ready to run! And she ran *everywhere*. After all, why walk when you can run? When she ran, her big, floppy ears streamed out behind her—so it looked just like she was flying!

It didn't matter if the sun was shining, the rain was pouring, or the snow was falling, Lucy-Lu loved being outside and playing with all the other dogs at her new home. She especially enjoyed being outside in the rain and the snow. If something wet was falling from the sky, she wanted to be out in it!

The Goodins made up for all those years without toys by making sure Lucy-Lu had all the playthings she wanted. Her favorite toys were big, hard rubber bones, which she chewed on to her heart's content. She always had to have one in her mouth. If Lucy-Lu wanted a drink of water, she simply dropped the bone she was carrying in the water dish. After taking a drink, she might leave the first bone there in the bowl and go off to find a different one. She had at least five different bones, including a pretty pink girly one, an Easter one, and an orange sporty one. Lucy-Lu had a bone for every occasion!

Belly Facials

Belly facials? That sounds kind of weird and . . . gross, doesn't it? But not to Lucy-Lu. You see, Belly was a little five-pound Peek-a-Pom who also lived with the Goodins. And Belly loved to lick faces. Michael and Zina called them "Belly facials." It was cute, but also a little icky.

Doggie Kisses

While it might seem a bit gross to us, licking is a sign of affection from a dog. It's like little doggie kisses.

For some reason, though, Lucy-Lu loved Belly. Perhaps it was because Belly was so small, and she reminded Lucy-Lu of all those puppies that had been taken away from her. Whatever the reason, Lucy-Lu would go up to Belly and talk to her. It wasn't exactly a bark. It was more of a *woo-woo-woo*. And it drove Belly crazy. That is, until one day when she realized, *I*

can lick this dog's face as much as I want! After that, the two dogs had a wonderful relationship. Lucy-Lu would *woo-woo-woo* at Belly, and Belly would lick Lucy-Lu's face.

The Beginning of a Dream

Lucy-Lu lived with Michael and Zina for over four years. While Lucy-Lu is no longer here to run through the yard, play in the snow, or get Belly facials, her joy lives on.

That's because Lucy-Lu inspired Zina and Michael to open Old Friends Senior Dog Sanctuary. When she jumped out of the car that first day and hit the yard smiling, the Goodins began to see that dogs with even the most terrible of pasts really could be rescued. With her ability to leave that basement behind and enjoy each new day, Lucy-Lu taught them that senior dogs still have so much life to live and so much love to give.

"These dogs can have the worst life ever," Zina says, "yet when they are rescued, they can leave all that behind and go on to have a good life. They deserve a chance to have that good life."

Even now, if asked to describe Lucy-Lu in one word, both Michael and Zina will say, "Happiness." Because happiness was what Lucy-Lu gave to them—and because of her, it's what the Goodins are now giving to hundreds of other old friends.

Meet Leo

BREED: chusky (a chow chow and Siberian husky mix)

AGE: about 14

SIZE: about 70 pounds, plus fur!

GENDER: male

LEO'S PEOPLE: Zina and Michael Goodin

FUN FACT

Did you know DNA tests exist for dogs? It turns out Leo is about 25 percent chow chow and 25 percent Siberian husky. The rest is a mix of Australian shepherd, English cocker spaniel, Shetland sheepdog, and Akita.

Off the Streets

The ground was hard and uncomfortable, but Leo hurt too much to move. So he didn't. He just lay there in the alley. Even when the nice-sounding men came out to look at him, he didn't move. For hours he just stayed right where he was, until a car drove up and a door opened.

Just a few hours before that, Zina and Michael got a phone call. It was from a friend who worked in a vet's office. Even though the Goodins had not yet started Old Friends, they already had a reputation as people who would rescue dogs.

"The lady told us that some guys had found a dog in the alley behind a barbershop on the other side of town," Zina remembers. "It was just lying there, not moving at all. They didn't want to call animal control because they knew that would turn out badly for the dog. 'Can you help him?' the lady asked us."

Zina didn't hesitate. "Sure!" she said. Zina and Michael jumped in the car and headed across town. They parked in front of the building and walked back to the alleyway. And there was Leo. His fur was clumped and full of huge mats. He was still alive, but he wasn't moving. Michael and Zina wondered how they would lift this big dog into their car. As it turned out, though, that was no problem at all.

Leo heard the car pull up close to him. He heard kind voices and people moving around. And then he heard the sound he had been waiting for: a car door opening. He lifted his head, pulled himself up to standing, and took off as fast as his aching legs could carry him—right into the back of the car. Leo didn't know where he was going, but he was sure it would be better than where he'd been.

The Lion

When Zina and Michael first found Leo back in 2012, they could tell he was in pain. He walked with a limp and had some bumps and tenderness, so they thought he might have been hit by a car. They also guessed that he had belonged to a homeless person and had then been left behind. The vet checked Leo out and took care of all of his medical needs. Then it was time to do *something* about all that fur.

The vet guessed that Leo was about eight years old when he was rescued from the streets. In all those years, it didn't seem that he had ever been brushed or groomed. His thick fur had matted into huge, painful clumps. Michael and Zina had no choice but to have him shaved. His first cut was a "lion cut"—which means most of his body was shaved except for a mane around his head and a fluffy tip on his tail.

And that's how he became "Leo the Lion."

Leo's lion cut caused a huge fuss though. While the sanctuary was still just a dream, Michael and Zina already had a Facebook following for their own senior dogs. And fans were not happy when Leo was shaved.

"Shaving Leo was actually the biggest uproar we ever had on Facebook," Zina says. "People would comment, 'You're not supposed to shave dogs. His hair will never grow back right.' But it always did. His hair was so thick, and Tennessee gets really hot. Leo was just so much happier in the summer after we shaved him. He would go outside more and play more. He would toss his head back and forth and *arrr, arrr, arrr*—just like a lion."

Even though Leo loved his lion cut, he hated getting it. His skin stayed tender his whole life, and he couldn't stand to be brushed. In fact, he had to be **sedated** in order to be groomed. For Leo's happiness and the groomer's safety, Leo was given medicine to make him sleep through the grooming. Because haircuts were so stressful for Leo—and because it's not good to sedate a dog too often—Michael and Zina only had him shaved once a year in the spring. His fur grew quickly (about one quarter inch a week), so he always had plenty of warm fur by the time cooler weather rolled around again.

A Star Is Born

So how did Leo the Lion become Leo the Rock Star? It all started with Facebook.

Zina began posting Leo's pictures on Facebook, along with their other dogs, and somehow his popularity just exploded. People fell in love with Leo, and somewhere along the way Leo the Rock Star was born. "He just had that look," Zina says. "He was very handsome."

Those were the early days when Michael and Zina were first making Old Friends into an official organization. Leo's Facebook fans helped them spread the word around the world about their mission to save senior dogs. A picture of Leo could easily get over 50,000 likes. Soon their followers were increasing by 100,000 people every month or so. Thanks in large part to Leo's fame, Old Friends now has over 1,800,000 Facebook

followers. The Goodins even made a shirt with Leo's picture on it—and sold over 25,000 of them!

Leo's fame hasn't been just on Facebook either. In true rock star fashion, Leo was one of the stars of the 2020 film *Seniors: A Dogumentary.*

AT HOME WITH A ROCK STAR

Even though Leo's Facebook fame helped start the sanctuary at GrandPaw's Gardens, he never lived there. Leo was always one of the "Home Gang"—the dogs who stay at home with Zina and Michael.

At the Goodins' home, Leo found other dogs to run and play with, all the food he could want, and—best of all—more love than he had ever known.

Like Lucy-Lu, Leo loved the snow. Some dogs won't even put their paws in the snow, but Leo couldn't get enough of it. Tennessee doesn't get a lot of snow, but whenever the flakes started falling, he would run outside to play and roll around in it. "I think it felt good to him," Zina says. "And I think he knew he looked good in the snow." A rock star *does* have to keep up his image.

Leo's fans always thought he was a teddy bear because of all his sweet pictures on Facebook. In real life, though, he sometimes demanded the rock star treatment. "He was really a great big baby," Zina remembers. "He was always super-sensitive. After he was groomed, I would have to sit up with him all night on the couch."

And Leo could be stubborn. "If you tried to put him on a leash and make him walk where he didn't want to go," Zina says, "it was like pulling a huge rock on a string. He was not going to budge. He wanted things his way."

Well, isn't that the way it's supposed to be when you're a rock star?

boof: a low, almost whispered bark

PAWSOME FACTS ABOUT LEO

- In spite of his rock star status, Leo got along well with other dogs at home. He never tried to hog the spotlight. He may have been called Leo the Lion, but he was actually a quiet leader. If another dog got out of line, he would simply give one low *boof!* and the other dog would instantly settle down.
- Leo's favorite spot to snooze was in a dog bed right next to Zina's side of the bed. If another of the dogs happened to beat him to that bed, Leo didn't make a fuss. He just moved in with the other dog.

- Toys weren't really Leo's thing. Being a rock star, he was above that sort of thing. Mostly he just enjoyed strolling around the yard. Zina once attached a GoPro camera to him to see all that Leo did—which was not a lot. He just slowly strutted around the yard, almost as if he were on parade for all his unseen, adoring Facebook fans.

Remembering the Rock Star

Leo lived the rock star life with Michael and Zina for six years. Then, in 2018, Leo slipped away in his sleep. He never got sick, and he never suffered. Fans from all over the world mourned his loss and celebrated his wonderful life.

At Old Friends, the loss of any dog is a sad time. Yet Zina and Michael and the rest of the Old Friends gang choose not to focus on the sadness of their loss. Rather, they remember the love and joy they were able to give Lucy-Lu and Leo and each of their other old friends. They think about the difference they made in the dogs' lives. And of course, they cherish the love and joy the dogs give back to them.

Both Lucy-Lu and Leo lived through some terrible times. But when they came home to Michael and Zina, both dogs were able to put their bad experiences behind them. They saw a chance to be happy, and they grabbed it with all four paws. Every pat, every treat, and *every* snowy day

was greeted with joy. Lucy-Lu and Leo didn't let the darkness of their pasts keep them from enjoying the new lives they were given. And that's definitely worth wagging a tail about!

MAVERICK AND MAISY

THE GENTLEMAN AND THE LADY

A SAD TALE

Maverick had been at the Old Friends sanctuary for months and months when he was fostered out to an older couple. At last he had found his home, and he was so happy! Then Maverick's people were in a terrible car accident, and the man died. Poor Maverick was heartbroken. He lay down outside the man's office door and grieved for his lost friend. Though the lady loved Maverick dearly, she was struggling to recover from the accident herself and could no longer take care of him.

BREED: Plott hound mix

AGE: about 10 years old

SIZE: about 70 pounds

GENDER: male

BREED: Labrador retriever mix

AGE: about 10 years old

SIZE: about 50 pounds

GENDER: female

MAVERICK AND MAISY'S PEOPLE: John and Melinda Knott

FUN FACT

If you pet Maisy, be prepared to give Maverick a pat or two. It's not that Maverick minds your petting Maisy—he just wants to make sure he gets his share!

The good news is that every old friend always has a place at the sanctuary. They *never* go back to an animal shelter. Maverick returned to Old Friends. Sadly, he didn't get along with some of the other dogs. He was an **alpha** dog and wanted to be the leader of the pack. But he wasn't the only dog who wanted to be the leader, and that's how the trouble started. To keep everyone peaceful, Maverick had to be rotated in and out of the play areas. He really needed a home of his own.

It was during Maverick's second stay at Old Friends that Maisy arrived. She had been rescued from a shelter. No one knows her history before the shelter, but Old Friends believes she lived on the streets for quite a while. Most of her teeth were already gone, and she was terribly underweight when she first came to the sanctuary. Her backbone and ribs poked up like the bars on a cage. The sanctuary began working right away to get her back to a healthy weight, giving her a careful mix of just the right foods in just the right amounts.

Both Maverick and Maisy had a sad tale, but it was about to take a much happier turn for both of them.

Nosing into a New Home

John and Melinda love old dogs. "Perhaps that's because we're old," Melinda says. This lively, retired couple had been without a dog for two years after the loss of their last four-legged friend. And they had been thinking it was time for them to find a new friend. The Knotts were looking at rescued Labradors when they found the Old Friends Senior Dog Sanctuary.

Love Never Grows Old

Senior dogs may be a bit older, but don't let their age fool you. They've still got lots of life to share. When these dogs find someone who's willing to treat them right and show them lots of love, they get a whole new "leash" on life. They can be as fun as puppies! In fact, they're often easier than puppies. Here are a few reasons why:

- A senior dog's personality is already set, so you know what kind of dog you're getting—whether it's a lapdog who always wants to be with you or a dog who likes to have time on its own.
- Many senior dogs are already house-trained.
- They're past that chew-everything-in-sight stage, so you don't have to watch them every second.
- You're still going to enjoy all the friendship of a dog, without some of the hassles.

Knowing what to expect is important when you're adopting or fostering any pet. If you're looking at adopting an older dog, remember . . .

- Seniors are still playful, but they don't have as much wild energy as puppies. This makes them great for families who don't have the time, space, or energy for lots of play.
- Senior dogs typically spend more time sleeping. This makes them great napping buddies!

- Some older dogs have come from rough backgrounds. Because of that, they may have some behaviors you'll have to work around. They may want to be the only dog in the house, not like tight spaces, be afraid of either men or women, or not like children. Be sure to spend time getting to know the dog before you take it home.
- Senior dogs may have some health troubles or need special medicine and treatments.

If your family is considering adopting a dog, don't just think about puppies. Consider an older dog. A senior dog will never grow too old for love. And the love you give that dog will be nothing compared to the love it will give you!

Because of its mission of saving seniors, they quickly decided the sanctuary was the place to look for a dog.

John and Melinda's search began with a trip to Old Friends to meet some of the dogs and perhaps choose one to be their next old friend. That's when they met Maisy. "She was such a sweet dog," Melinda says. "The other dogs would almost push her out of the way to get to us, but she was so gentle."

Melinda and John fell in love with Maisy. But on that same trip, Maverick decided John was the person for him.

Maverick followed his every step and kept nosing in to be close to him. After learning Maverick's story, John thinks he knows why: "Maverick had bonded to his first foster dad, who was an older gentleman. So it just made sense that he would attach himself to me." John laughs. "I guess I was the first old man he had run across since then."

There was only one problem—the Knotts had already agreed to take Maisy. The paperwork was filled out, and they were headed home to prepare. They would need a bed, bowls for food and water, a leash—and, of course, toys. But the couple only made it about halfway home when they realized they couldn't let Maverick stay at the sanctuary. As soon as they got home, they called Old Friends and said, "We want them both!" They were going to need twice as many beds, bowls, leashes, and toys, but the Knotts didn't mind a bit. "We couldn't wait to get those dogs," Melinda says. But first, Old Friends needed to do a home visit. A staff member always visits every new home to make sure all is safe and good for the dogs. Melinda remembers, "So I told them, 'How about right now?'" After the inspection was complete, it was time to bring Maverick and Maisy home.

Because Maverick was the bigger dog and liked to be the leader, Old Friends suggested they bring him home first and let him establish his turf. When the Knotts came to pick Maverick up, the whole staff stepped out to say goodbye. That was the Wednesday before Thanksgiving. Sally,

one of the Old Friends staff, said, "This is the best Christmas present I could have—to get a home for Maverick."

Now you might be wondering how a rescue dog behaved in a new home full of Thanksgiving guests *and* a great, big roasted turkey. "He was so good," Melinda says. "He was a perfect gentleman. He didn't even beg at the table."

The next week, John and Melinda went back to pick up Maisy—who has turned out to be quite the lady. Maisy and Maverick have been together ever since!

The Adventures of Maverick and Maisy

A day with Maverick and Maisy around is never going to be dull. But these two old friends like to start their days in *very* different ways.

Maverick loves to sleep in and practically has to be dragged out of bed. No one can move as slow as Maverick in the morning!

Maisy, on the other hand—*er*, paw—is a chatterbox in the mornings. She may not say much the whole rest of the day, but in the mornings this lady just talks and talks. *Aroo-roo-roo-roo-roo. Aroo-roo.* There's a whole conversation happening every morning, as far as Maisy is concerned anyway. And she keeps right on talking until breakfast is served.

Chow Time!

Maisy may be missing most of her teeth, but she doesn't let that slow her down when it's time to eat. She has no trouble chowing down on her kibble mixed with just a bit of canned food to make it extra tasty. Maisy is still on a special diet to try to get her weight back up to a healthy level, but she never has to worry about going hungry again.

Maverick has plenty of teeth and is definitely *not* a picky eater. In fact, he'll eat just about anything. Except lettuce. Maverick *hates* lettuce. He's great at licking plates clean though. Who need a dishwasher with Maverick around?

Who Wants to Play?

When it's time to play, Maverick will tell you there's no better game than "Pull" (or tug-of-war). In fact, just say the word "pull," and Maverick will head for his toy box to dig out his favorite rope. If John and Melinda aren't up for a game of Pull, then Maverick will grab his stuffed hedgehog. He'll toss his head to send it flying through the air and chomp on it to make the squeaker "grunt." If John and Melinda hear a big noise crashing through the living room, they know it's probably just Maverick playing with his hedgehog.

As for Maisy, she's much too ladylike to care much about toys or games. She's just happy being Maisy. "If you throw something for her to fetch," Melinda says, "she just looks at you like, 'You threw it, you go get it.'"

Maverick and Maisy have their own toy box in the living room, and it's filled with toys, which they—well, mostly Maverick—definitely know how to pull out. "We're still working on putting the toys back in the box though," Melinda says.

Oh well, even dogs can't be perfect, right?

Who Gets the Comfy Couch?

After an exhausting game of "toss the hedgehog" or "just being Maisy," this pair needs a nap. According to both dogs, the best napping spot in the house is the couch. And it can be a bit of a race to see who gets it.

If John and Melinda aren't home or are in another room, Maisy will sometimes get on the couch first and refuse to let Maverick up there. She'll curl her lip and snarl at him. The funny thing is, she can't really do anything because she has no teeth! Yet Maisy's don't-mess-with-me attitude is enough to convince Maverick that curling up in John's chair will work just fine.

If the Knotts are close by, however, Maverick pretty much owns the couch. They'll have Maisy get down so Maverick can have his couch. "After all, he was here first," Melinda says. But Maverick lives up to his nickname of "Gentleman." Once he's comfy on the couch, Maisy will sometimes join him, and that's just fine with Maverick.

I'm the Leader! Aren't I?

True to his alpha-dog personality, Maverick likes to be the in-charge dog. And Maisy sometimes lets him *think* he is. For example, when they're out on their daily walk, Maverick insists on being the lead dog. If Maisy gets ahead of him, he'll quickly trot up in front of her. He doesn't have to be way ahead; just a nose in front will do. And Maisy . . . well, a lady has more important things to worry about, right?

In fact, Maisy is very laid-back. She has the sweetest personality, and not much ruffles her feathers. *Except* when it comes to the couch or when Maverick walks too close to her favorite purple pillow. *That's* a different story. When Maisy curls her lips and gives her best back-off snurl, Maverick follows directions and backs away.

Like all great leaders, Maverick knows when it's time to let someone else be in charge.

Good Night, Maverick and Maisy

After a day filled with adventures, every dog needs a good night's sleep. On Maverick's first night with the Knotts, he climbed up on the bed and crawled right up between them. It took a little coaching, but now Maverick knows his spot is on his blanket at the end of the bed. "John was always so strict about not letting animals on the furniture." Melinda laughs. "Now guess who has his own blanket on our bed?"

As soon as it's bedtime, Maverick hops right up on his

blanket. “But,” John warns, “if you get up for any reason, Maverick will move up and take your spot!”

Maisy doesn’t care to sleep on the bed. In fact, she doesn’t seem to care where she sleeps. Any comfy spot will do, though you’ll often find her on the couch. Even though she doesn’t care about sleeping in the bed, she does sometimes enjoy messing with Maverick. She’ll block his path to the bed and dare him to try to get past her. That’s when John and Melinda have to step in and clear a path for Maverick to get on the bed. Because even though Maverick is bigger, he does not mess with Maisy.

Pawsome Facts About Maverick and Maisy

- Maverick loves chasing squirrels. He can spot a squirrel high up in a tree long before John or Melinda sees it. Then he’ll run over to the tree and stand at attention, pointing right up at it and baying, *Aroo-roo-roo!* In fact, Maverick bays at just about anything that moves—birds, deer, or whatever critters he happens to see.
- If you open a car door, be ready for Maisy to jump right in. She’s always ready to go for a ride!
- One of Maisy’s favorite sprawling spots is the rug in the middle of the kitchen floor. It can make cooking a bit tough, but the Knotts agree she’s worth working around.

- Maverick loves kids and is so gentle with them. When kids walk up, he sits and lets them climb all over him.
- Maisy shows her affection with dainty, ladylike kisses. If she likes you, Maisy will come right up to your face and plant a tiny, quick kiss on your chin or hand.

What Is a Plott Hound?

Plott hounds were first bred in America in the 1700s. Johannes Plott brought five German "Hanover hounds" with him when he moved to North Carolina in 1750. His family bred those dogs with local mountain dogs. The result was called the Plott hound. These hardworking dogs were used to hunt bears and wild boar. Though they can be fierce hunters, they are known for being well behaved, gentle, and loyal at home.

More Adventures Coming Soon!

John and Melinda have even more fun plans for Maverick and Maisy. When the weather warms, Maverick and Maisy will get to go on their first trip to a campground. It's a huge area that's all fenced in but filled with woods and fields for them to run through. John and Melinda have played hide-and-seek there with their other dogs in the past. "Where's Gigi? Where's Papi?" they'd call as the dogs scrambled to find them. There's also a path for Maverick and Maisy to follow that leads to a beautiful, clear lake, where they'll be able to cool off from their adventures with a swim.

The Jackpot

Maverick's and Maisy's eyes shine like stars with the wonder of finding such an amazing forever home. "These dogs are so loving," Melinda says. "They want to please you. They want to do what you want them to do. They are just so grateful and happy to be here—right from the start. That's one of the things we love about older dogs and especially shelter dogs. It's like they know they've got something special going."

"We feel like we hit the jackpot with Mav and Maisy," says John.

And from the way their tails are wagging, it's clear that Maverick and Maisy feel the same way.

MARCO

THE BIG TEDDY BEAR

At Old Friends, the staff is used to dealing with all kinds of dogs and their personalities. They don't scare easily. But *everyone* was afraid of Marco. Then came Robert. With a little patience and a lot of love, everything changed for Marco, who—as it turns out—is just a big teddy bear.

BREED: Belgian Malinois and German shepherd mix

AGE: between 8 and 10 years old

SIZE: about 80 pounds

GENDER: male

MARCO'S PERSON: Robert Hatter

FUN FACT

Marco loves to sing. Anytime an ambulance, fire truck, or police car goes by with its sirens blazing, Marco raises his head and sings . . . *er*, howls . . . along. And he's always in perfect tune! He even sings along with the sirens on TV.

Out of a Hurricane

Marco first came to the sanctuary as part of a group of rescues from Florida during Hurricane Irma in 2017. The shelters in the path of the hurricane needed to move their animals north—not only for their safety, but also to make room for other animals lost during the storm. And that's about all the people at Old Friends know about his past.

When he first came, sanctuary workers thought Marco was a senior dog. But after a while they figured out he was only about six or seven years old. Since all of the other dogs at the sanctuary are seniors and move a bit slower, Marco's energy and bouncing around caused some problems with the other dogs.

Marco was also a **resource guarder**. That means he was fiercely protective of his things, including his food, his bowls, and his toys. If anyone—dog or human—tried to get near anything of his, he would snarl and snap and probably bite. He was a scary dog. And Marco was big and strong, which made him even scarier.

To protect the workers and other dogs, as well as Marco himself, he was put into **isolation**. Of all the dogs at the sanctuary, only about ten are put into isolation in their own rooms. And while that may seem sad, it's so much better than at a shelter where dogs with these kinds of struggles are usually put to sleep. Marco had his own space. He got to play outside and go for walks. But he couldn't be trusted out in the garden with the other dogs. For two long years, Marco stayed in isolation . . . until Robert came to work at the sanctuary.

Robert to the Rescue

Robert began working at Old Friends in June 2019. And despite Marco's reputation as a dog to be feared, the first time Robert saw him, he fell in love with the big guy.

"When I first started working there," Robert says, "he was already in isolation. I would just stop by his space and say hi. I wouldn't mess with his stuff or anything. But right from the start, he treated me a little differently than anyone else. He seemed to trust me, and over time, he began to warm up to me. Very slowly I worked up to touching his bowl. He didn't growl or bark. He kind of looked at me, but he let me do it. After that we bonded really quickly. Marco picked me just as much as I picked Marco. He loved being around me, and I loved being around him."

How Old?

Most of the dogs at Old Friends are at least ten years old. But the sanctuary rarely knows the exact age of the dogs it rescues. After all, you can't exactly ask them when their birthday is!

So how do sanctuary workers guess a dog's age? Mostly by their teeth. Puppies, of course, will still have their baby teeth. But with older dogs, it's often just a guess. The younger a dog is, the more bumps and ridges its teeth will have. After years of chewing, these bumps and ridges grind down. The smoother a dog's teeth are, then, the more likely it is to be older. But if a dog isn't healthy or has lived as a stray on the streets, its teeth—and the rest of it!—can sometimes be in bad shape. This makes the dog appear older than it really is. That's how younger dogs sometimes end up at Old Friends.

It didn't take long for Robert to know that Marco was the dog for him. Even though he worked at Old Friends, Robert still went through the application and home inspection to become a forever foster. And then, at long last, it was time for Marco to get a forever home of his own.

Robert loaded Marco into his car after work and headed toward home. Marco seemed to think that ride in the car was the best thing he'd ever done. He was thrilled! First, he'd sit up and look all around at the cars and trees and buildings passing by. Then he'd lay down for a bit—only to pop back up again a minute later. There was just so much to see and smell! When at last they reached Robert's house, Marco trotted right in the front door and ran from room to room. He checked out every single inch of the entire house and all around the backyard, sniffing everything as he went.

At first, Robert was a little worried about what Marco might tear up in the house. At Old Friends, he was famous for shredding toys and blankets. The staff even gave Robert some old things that Marco could tear up. But the first time Marco started ripping up a blanket, Robert just looked at him and said, "No." Marco stared up at Robert with those big eyes, as if to say, "Oh, okay." He instantly stopped shredding the blanket and has never torn anything up again.

The best thing about Marco's new home has been the way it has changed his whole personality. He isn't protective of his food or toys anymore. He doesn't growl or bite. He's now the gentlest, calmest dog you could imagine. Marco's

days are filled with running, playing, eating, and sleeping—everything a dog needs for a happy life.

"He's home here," Robert says. "He knows we're pals."

Just a Big Goofball

Marco might look serious, and everyone might have thought he was the bad boy of the sanctuary, but these days? He can be downright goofy! Like when someone knocks on the front door. Marco gets so excited and scrambles to get to the door as fast as he can—so fast that he often slides right past it on the hardwood floors, much like a character in a cartoon.

If something catches Marco's attention, he'll look up and his ears—which are *huge*—will pop straight up, just like a bunny's ears. And that's how he got his nickname: "Bunny Rabbit." Since carrots are also one of his favorite foods, his nickname is an extra-good fit. And you'll never guess what one of his favorite things to do is. This tough guy is a sucker for watching butterflies outside the window!

There's only one thing that really upsets Marco these days, and it's actually kind of funny. This big dog with his rough reputation is absolutely *terrified* of tiny dogs. In fact, if he's out on a walk with Robert and spots a tiny dog, Marco will practically drag Robert to the other side of the street to escape.

And speaking of walks . . .

W-A-L-K AND T-R-E-A-T

Marco is one smart fellow. Robert has quickly learned that he needs to spell certain words so Marco won't get too excited. Like w-a-l-k. The instant Marco hears the word *walk* or hears the click of his leash, he takes off for the front door like a lightning bolt. Marco is always up for a walk around the neighborhood—unless he can talk Robert into a run. Of course, he can run around in his fenced-in backyard anytime he wants, but a long run with Robert is even better.

T-r-e-a-t is another word that's best to spell. Unless, of course, you're ready to hand over a yummy treat. Marco doesn't get a lot of treats, though he does love Milk-Bones. One of Robert's friends once gave him some duck jerky made for dogs. *That* was gobbled up in an instant!

Every evening Marco looks forward to his "night-night treat." It's really one of those special bones that cleans a dog's teeth, but—*shhh!*—Marco doesn't know that. Though he can't read a clock, somehow Marco knows when it's eight o'clock and time for his night night treat. He'll lie in front of the cupboard where they're kept and look at Robert, as if to say, *Hey! Don't you know what time it is? It's treat time!*

W-a-l-k and t-r-e-a-t . . . the only trouble with all of this spelling is that Marco is starting to figure it all out. Who knew dogs could learn to spell?

Ruffhousing with Marco

One of the greatest things Marco has learned since coming home with Robert is how to play. He's no longer the scary, big guy guarding his toys. Now he's the big goofball handing you toys to play with—he especially loves to share his rope for a game of tug-of-war. He'll even be silly sometimes and roll over to let you rub his belly, with his tail wagging like crazy the whole time.

Marco's most favorite game is wrestling. All Robert has to do is put his hand on Marco's paw. That's the signal to start. Marco will give a little play growl—*grrr, grrr*—and then it's on! Down on the floor, rolling over, chasing around and around, with arms, legs, and paws everywhere! There are even times when Marco starts up a match. If Robert is busy doing something else and Marco wants to wrestle, he'll put his paw on Robert and do his little *grrr, grrr* growl to tell him, *It's time for a match!*

Marco the Teddy Bear

Marco also shares his new sense of playfulness with others. The kids in the neighborhood just love him. Every school day, a bus stops right outside Marco's home at 7:20 a.m., and Marco is right there every morning to see the kids off with a goodbye bark. Some of the kids even give him a big wave back.

What Is a Belgian Malinois?

Belgian Malinois are known for being smart. They love to stay active, and they love to be with their people. Mals, as they are sometimes called, were first bred to be herding dogs for sheep and cattle.

These days, you'll often find Mals working as police and military dogs. There was even a Malinois named Cairo who was part of SEAL Team Six and helped take down one of the world's worst terrorists: Osama bin Laden. Military dogs like Cairo are each given their own body armor and night-vision goggles. Because of their excellent sniffing skills, they are often used to search for drugs and bombs. You'll even find Mals guarding the White House!

What Is a German Shepherd?

German shepherds are one of the best worker dogs. They are brave and loyal to their owners, even defending them with their own lives! Like the Malinois, they were first bred as herders. These dogs are also extremely smart and quick to learn. You'll find German shepherds serving as guide dogs, working with police officers, and serving with the military.

At Halloween, Robert set up a kiddie gate in front of the door so Marco could greet all of the kids who came trick-or-treating. The little ones would come up and wrap their arms around him—and that big teddy bear loved every moment of it.

What a Second Chance Can Do

When Marco was at the sanctuary, he growled and snapped at anyone who came too close. No one would have ever guessed he could change so much. Gone is the dog who guarded his food. Gone is the dog who shredded blankets and ripped up toys. Now that he is safe in his own home with no worries or fears, Marco is free to be the big, lovable goofball of a dog he was always meant to be. Which just goes to show what a second chance and a good dose of love and kindness can do.

"Marco has a whole new life now," Robert says. "He's just a big teddy bear. Marco has learned to be comfortable just being his own goofball self."

BUDDY

MR. EYES TO THE SKIES

Dogs are just so easy to love. Well, most of them. Some dogs can be a bit tougher to get close to. But every dog deserves a chance to be loved. And for Buddy, a little love made all the difference.

BREED: German shepherd mix

AGE: 15

SIZE: 85 pounds

GENDER: male

BUDDY'S PEOPLE: Kay and Wendell Norman

FUN FACT

Buddy's most favorite thing to do was bark. And he was *really* good at it.

A Home at Last

Like many of the dogs at Old Friends, no one knows much about Buddy's history. He came to the sanctuary in 2015 as a rescue from a shelter. He was very anxious and had a hard time getting along with other dogs. He was also a constant barker. Seriously, Buddy barked at pretty much everything, including the air. Buddy barked *all the time*.

Because of these challenges, Buddy was not a good fit for staying at the sanctuary, where the dogs live together in social groups. Fortunately Old Friends works with a pet-boarding business, and Buddy was able to stay there. He had his own space to run, and he could bark as much as he liked.

That worked great for a few months. Then Christmastime

rolled around, and the boarding business needed all its space for customers. Buddy would have to leave for at least a couple of weeks. Where could Buddy stay?

Zina turned to Kay, one of the Old Friends volunteers. Zina knew that Kay and her husband, Wendell, had had German shepherds before. "Do you think you can take him?" Zina asked.

Kay and Wendell talked about it and decided to give it a try. "But he has to be nice to my other dogs," Kay said. At that time they had another old friend living with them, a cocker spaniel. And they also had a little, twenty-five-pound terrier named Pippin.

Well, as it turned out, Buddy *was* nice to Kay and Wendell's other dogs. In fact, Buddy liked both of them, and both dogs liked him. Buddy also liked Kay and Wendell. They never really figured out what made Buddy like them and their dogs when he didn't like so many others. They all just clicked together like the pieces of a puzzle. Whatever the reason, Buddy was happy, and so Kay and Wendell were happy. When the Christmas break ended, it was time to send Buddy back to boarding. But Kay told Zina, "Just let him stay here. Don't send him back." Buddy had found a forever home.

bork: another word for *bark*. Some people say the sound a dog makes is more like *bork!* than *bark!* What do you think?

Through the Woods

Buddy was thrilled to live with Kay and Wendell. He had a huge, fenced-in backyard to run in. Behind the yard was an even bigger forest area that was also fenced in. Buddy and his new friend Pippin could run and explore and sniff to their hearts' content.

Sometimes Pippin would grab a toy and run with it, and Buddy would chase him. For the most part, though, Buddy didn't care much for balls or toys himself. In fact, if you threw a ball for him, he would just look at it as if to say, *Nah, I don't want to go get that.* Then he'd trot off to find something to bark at.

Because barking was what Buddy loved best. At the Normans' house, neighbors were few and far between. So Buddy could *bark, bark, bark* all he wanted. Which was a good thing, because Buddy wasn't about to give up his barking. He barked at everything. *EVERYTHING.* Cars driving by on the road, leaves falling to the ground, birds flying over the yard.

And speaking of birds . . .

Look to the Skies!

Buddy was fascinated with flying things. He would run across the backyard with his head up, searching the skies,

just barking and having the best time. Kay says, "It was like he was searching for enemy airplanes or something."

Buddy especially loved to bark at the birds. Just let some big bird fly over the yard, and he would go crazy, following it as far as he could and barking the whole way.

One day Kay heard a terrible barking out in the woods. After a while, an owner gets to know their dog's bark. They can often tell when a dog is happy, hungry, or scared just by the different sounds it makes.

"I could tell it was a different sort of bark," Kay says. "I knew Buddy and Pippin had something." And boy, did they ever. A young buzzard had gotten inside the fence. It was flapping its wings like crazy, and Buddy was dancing and barking all around it. Kay helped the bird get outside the fence. But for Buddy, that was the thrill of his life: one of those big flying things had actually come down to see him!

The Ultimate Guard Dog

Though Buddy loved Kay and Wendell, he never really learned to care for anyone else. That made him the ultimate guard dog. He would not let anybody else come into the house or yard.

Buddy was not messing around either. He could get very aggressive. Kay quickly learned that whenever a visitor came to the house, Buddy had to be put in her office. (Fortunately, Kay's office was also Buddy's favorite napping spot, so he didn't mind too much.)

One day, though, a young man came to do some yard work—and Buddy escaped! Buddy went after him, and that young man jumped a five-foot fence in a single bound, just like a pole vaulter. Kay later told him, "That was amazing! I'm impressed!"

These days Kay has a female old friend who looks a bit like Buddy. She also is a bit of a guard dog. When she sees that same young man working in the yard, she barks and growls just as if she were going to eat him up. But she's much smaller, and he just laughs at her. "I've met the real thing," he tells her, "and I'm not afraid of you." He's nicknamed her "Buddy Jr."

Pawsome Facts About Buddy

- Buddy's favorite sleeping spot was the giant dog mattress in Kay's office. He slept there at night and napped there any time Kay was nearby. He just loved that bed and being with Kay.
- Buddy also loved to lie in the den, where he could see out the door and watch the birds and squirrels outside. And, of course, bark at them.
- Some dogs always love to be petted, but not Buddy. He

would let you know when he wanted to be loved on. And when he did, there was no special spot. Ears, head, chest—he loved it all! Once in a while, he would even roll over for a tummy rub—the ultimate sign of trust from a dog.

New Tricks

Just because a senior dog is older—and probably a bit slower—that doesn't mean it's going to be like a stuffed animal that flops on the bed or couch. *All* dogs love to go for walks and to play with their friends. People are often surprised by just how much life and energy senior dogs have left in them.

Another surprising thing is how good senior dogs are at learning new things. For example, the Normans' home has a dog door, and every dog they've ever had has learned to use it. Some of them learn in just a minute or two; others take a week or two. But they all learn. They learn where they're supposed to eat and where they're supposed to sleep. The dogs settle into the routine of the family very quickly.

One lesson all of the Normans' dogs must learn is to wait at the gate. Because the road is nearby, it's important that the dogs don't rush out of the gate as soon as Kay opens it. She doesn't want them running into the road where they could be hurt. So each of the dogs learns to wait. That just proves that you really can teach an old dog new tricks.

It's not just the dogs who learn a new trick or two. Kay and Wendell discovered that opening up your home to old dogs can be just as rewarding for you as it is for the dogs. From her work at the sanctuary, Kay knows that some people worry whether an old dog will ever forget about whoever or whatever was in the past. And they wonder if the dog will be able to love again. But she says, "These dogs will absolutely adore you." Once a dog feels safe, it will bond to you quickly. It will love you and be loyal to you.

People will sometimes ask Kay, "Why do you keep taking in old dogs who won't live as long as puppies would? Why do you put yourself through that?" Kay's answer is this:

"We believe that every living creature deserves to live a safe, peaceful life surrounded by love. By giving hope and happiness to senior dogs, we make our own lives richer. Each of these dogs is a gift that lives on in our hearts long after they are gone."

"My Buddy Lesson"

Buddy first came to stay with Kay and Wendell in December 2015, and he lived with them for two years. Then, in 2017, his body just gave out. But oh, what a wonderful two years those were for Buddy! He had all the love, running, and barking he wanted.

"Buddy was the first dog that I felt like I really made a difference at the end of his life," says Kay. "If he hadn't come to live here, he would have lived the rest of his life in that boarding place.

"All these sweet little dogs around the sanctuary—someone will take them. But nobody would have taken Buddy. I'm so grateful that I had Buddy early on because I learned from him that I can love any dog. I really can. And any dog is going to respond to that love.

"That was my Buddy lesson."

Kay continues, "Every old friend we have had has been one that I have been asked to take. I don't come in and say I'm in love with this dog or that dog. When one old friend passes on, I say, 'Who most needs a home?'"

Buddy started that. Every dog Kay has taken in since has had troubles—either medical troubles or behavior troubles. Kay understands that some dogs just don't do well in the sanctuary with lots of other dogs around. But when they get into a home with no other dogs around or just one or two other dogs, they blossom. No matter what they've been through, in the right environment and with someone who has the patience to work with them, they will do well.

Buddy never did get over his fierceness with strangers. He never stopped barking at every bird in the sky. And he never stopped chasing the yard man whenever he got the

chance. But he was able to live out his life in a safe place with people who knew how to take care of him.

He was happy. He was loved. And love will always make a difference.

CHESTNUT

THE WONDER DOG

At first glance, you might think Chestnut is just another dog. But this is no ordinary dog. He's Chestnut—the laundry-loving, goal-scoring, on-the-job wonder dog. And he's sure to steal your heart . . . along with your snacks!

BREED: hound mix

AGE: about 10 to 12 years old

SIZE: about 30 pounds

GENDER: male

CHESTNUT'S PEOPLE: Brandi, Brent, and Jack Fruin

FUN FACT

Unlike most dogs, Chestnut doesn't care for popcorn or pretzels. Instead he *loves* broccoli and Caesar salad.

Why Not?

Brandi grew up in Mt. Juliet, so she first discovered Old Friends when one of their posts popped up on her Facebook feed one day. She clicked on it and fell in love with the sanctuary's mission of taking in the often-forgotten older dogs. She's been following them online ever since.

Soon Brandi was showing pictures of the dogs to her husband, Brent, and their son, Jack, who's now twelve. "It's one of our favorite things to do," Brandi says, "look at old friends on social media. We love to keep up with the dogs, even though we don't know them."

One of Jack's favorite dogs to watch was a little tan-and-white, droopy-eared beagle named Charlie Brown. When Charlie Brown got a foster home of his own, it was wonderful news for him, but Jack needed to find a new friend to watch. Not long after that, the family started seeing this little brown dog who loved to lie on top of one of the couches at the sanctuary. He would stare out the window, almost as if he were looking for someone to take him home. His name was Chestnut.

"The first time I saw him," Jack says, "I thought, *He's just the cutest dog*. He was very shy and wouldn't look at the camera. He just stared off into the distance like a little old man."

Jack actually followed Chestnut online for quite a while. The family already had two beagles, and they weren't planning on getting another dog. But they kept seeing Chestnut, and they found themselves talking about him more and more. Then one day, they said, "Why not? Let's get him!" And that's exactly what they did.

They filled out the paperwork and were visited by the Old Friends staff to make sure their home would be a good fit for Chestnut. When all was approved, they drove straight to the sanctuary and scooped him up. That was February 22, 2018—Chestnut's Gotcha Day. Chestnut has been with the Fruins over two years now, and they celebrate each Gotcha Day with a special treat and, of course, lots of extra kisses and cuddles.

What Is a Bloodhound?

The bloodhound is sometimes called the "sleuth hound." This breed is famous for its super-sharp sense of smell. These hounds are often used to track down people—whether it's lost children or hikers or a criminal trying to hide from police. Evidence from a bloodhound's tracking can even be used in court! There's not another animal, man, or machine that can track as well as the bloodhound.

What Is a Vizsla?

The vizsla is also called a Hungarian pointer. This breed can trace its roots all the way back to the tenth century. By the 1700s and 1800s, the modern vizsla dog was being bred as a hunting dog for nobles and warlords. They became famous for being able to do just about anything they were asked to do—from hunting to being a jogging partner for morning runs.

Feels Like Home

No one knows much about Chestnut's life before the sanctuary, but his life after Old Friends has been nothing but the very best. From day one, Chestnut seemed to know that he was home. "He acts like he's always been here," Brent says.

The very first night, when it was time for sleep, Brent put Chestnut up in Jack's bed. About ten minutes later, Chestnut started down the stairs. Brent simply said, "That's your brother. You sleep with him." Chestnut turned right around and went back to Jack, as if he had perfectly understood every single word. (Which, of course, he surely did.)

And that's still where he sleeps each night . . . unless Brandi and Brent steal him from Jack. Wait. What would prompt parents to steal a pup from their own son? Well, you see, Chestnut is a plopper.

The Chestnut Plop

Chestnut does this wonderful thing when he's ready to sleep. He picks out his spot, settles into position, and then—*plops*. Hard! It's almost as if his legs suddenly give out. Brent, Brandi, and Jack call it the "Chestnut Plop."

"So we'll be in bed," Brandi says, "and we'll say, 'Give us a plop! Give us a plop!' And he'll do it. He'll just plop down next to you. Chestnut doesn't like to lie *on* you, but rather right up against you. The weight is so soothing. It's like this calm feeling just comes over you. That's why we steal him from Jack sometimes. Because the Chestnut Plop is just so *delicious*!"

"We don't need those weighted blankets," Jack says, who's been known to steal him back. "We have a Chestnut blanket."

Where's Alice?

Chestnut's neighbor for the first year in his forever home was an older lady named Alice. While Chestnut would have loved to be her friend, Alice was not really a dog person.

That didn't stop Chestnut from hanging out with Alice though—at least in his own way. "Our living room window is right across from her sunroom window," Brent explains. "So while we were away at work and school, Chestnut would keep an eye on Alice's comings and goings all day long."

The family didn't realize how much their neighbor meant to Chestnut until Alice became sick and had to leave her home. Chestnut mourned for days. He would sit at the window and bark as if to say, "Where's Alice?"

Now that some new neighbors have moved in, Chestnut is much happier. He loves "hanging out" and keeping an eye on them too.

Hey, I'm People Too!

Chestnut considers himself one of the family—and not a four-legged member either! In fact, if the Fruins try to put

him out in the backyard with the other dogs to play for a bit, he barks and barks as if to say, "I'm not a dog! Let me back in!" Chestnut prefers the house and the front yard—you know, where all the other people are.

And he always wants to be near his people. He doesn't care to be in their laps, like a lot of dogs. But he does want to be where he can keep an eye on them. "He'll follow your every step," Brandi says, "from room to room, especially if there is only one of us at home. It's very sweet."

This isn't just a daytime thing either. Chestnut seems to think of himself as the family's security guard. He patrols the house in the middle of the night to make sure everyone is in bed, where they're supposed to be. Brent travels for work and sometimes has to leave late at night. First, though, he has to check in with Chestnut and make sure the dog sees him leave. Otherwise, Chestnut will bark to alert the rest of the family that Brent is missing during the nightly bed check.

The Fruins know they'd better be on their toes when Chestnut is on duty. But security guard isn't Chestnut's only job.

ON THE JOB!

Chestnut isn't just around for his great looks and plopping—he's got a job to do. And he takes it very seriously. Every day he walks Jack to school. "He just prances up the sidewalk," Brent says. "It's like he's been doing this his whole life, and this is what he's here for: to escort Jack to school."

Rainy days can be a bit of a challenge. That's because Chestnut absolutely hates walking in the rain. To solve that problem, the Fruins bought him his own special dog umbrella. It's like a regular umbrella, except the handle comes out of the top so the umbrella part can be held down over the dog.

Rain or shine, when Chestnut is on the job, he doesn't tolerate tardiness. If Brent and Jack haven't left for school by seven thirty in the morning, Chestnut will start barking. Most afternoons Chestnut walks back over with Brent to pick up Jack at the end of the school day. So he'll bark again at about two thirty to remind Brent that it's time to get a move on.

In fact, it's quite amazing how Chestnut seems to be able to tell time. Which is great—except on weekends, or summers, or Christmas break. He doesn't seem to understand why these days are different. So don't expect to sleep in on a Saturday when Chestnut's on the job!

It's not just the family that Chestnut likes to keep on schedule. He also knows exactly when soccer practice should end. If it gets to be 7:03 p.m. and Coach is still going, Chestnut will bark to tell him, *Come on, Coach! It's time to go!* Coach just laughs and says, "Okay, Chestnut! I guess it's time to wrap it up."

The School Celebrity

Chestnut is something of a celebrity at Jack's school. He even got his picture taken for the first day of school. All the kids love to come up and pet him. How does Chestnut handle all the attention? He just sits quietly and stares calmly off into the distance. After all, dealing with your adoring fans is all part of being a celebrity, right?

Once a week, Brent helps with the car line at school, and Chestnut is right by his side. All the other dogs in the cars bark their hellos to him. Chestnut is usually too busy keeping everyone moving to bark back though. Remember, he's got a job to do!

The Wonder Dog

When Chestnut first came to live with them, the Fruins thought he was about ten years old. But he's so nimble, they wonder if he's not a bit younger. The first time they left him at home, they put him in the kitchen with a baby gate because they weren't sure if he would tear things up around the house. Well, that didn't work. Chestnut instantly leaped over the gate in a single bound! Next they tried putting the gate at the top of the stairs so he would have the whole upstairs to himself. Again he jumped right over the gate, this time landing perfectly on the stairs. Needless to say, Chestnut now has the run of the house.

Chestnut has also figured out how to jump up on the kitchen counter—just like a cat. (But don't tell *him* that!) The family quickly learned to be careful about what they left out on the counters. Plastic baggies and even screw-on lids are no match for this wonder dog. "He'll just eat what he wants," Brandi says. "Then he'll look at you like, 'Oh, you wanted those? Well, I ate them.'"

"When we leave, he watches at the door," Brent says. "Sometimes I think he's sad, but other times I think he's just waiting until we're gone so he can go check out the kitchen. A couple of times, I've come back for something, and he's already in the kitchen." He's probably investigating whatever is in that plastic baggie.

Chestnut for the Goal

Kitchen counters aren't the only place Chestnut likes to show off his skills. Soccer is Jack's game, and since Chestnut is one of his biggest fans, he loves to be on the field with Jack. While Chestnut enjoys running with Jack and his friends, playing with the ball isn't really his thing. If it gets passed to him, he usually runs away. After all, the ball is almost as big as he is!

"But there was one time," Jack says, "I was playing

with some friends, and the ball got kicked toward him. Chestnut arched his back up at the perfect moment, and the ball bounced off him into the goal." *GOOOAAALLL!* Another time, Chestnut blocked a goal. It happened when Chestnut was standing in front of the goal, and one of Jack's friends tried to chip the ball over him because he didn't want to hit him. Chestnut barely nudged the ball as it went by and sent the ball sailing past the goal. That's a save for Chestnut!

PAWSOME FACTS ABOUT CHESTNUT

- Even though Chestnut doesn't care for the rain, he actually *likes* taking a bath. Go figure!
- Chestnut loves warm laundry. Brandi will dump the laundry out on the bed to fold it, and before she knows it, Chestnut has *plopped* right in the middle of it.
- Speaking of clothes, Chestnut is something of a clothes hound. He has sweaters for every day, bunny ears for Easter, and a Santa outfit for Christmas.
- Chestnut's absolute favorite hobby is sleeping. The very best spot for a daytime nap is the couch, but first he has to make it *just right*. That means knocking off all of the pillows and blankets before plopping down. His other favorite spot to snooze is in a patch of sunshine on the floor.

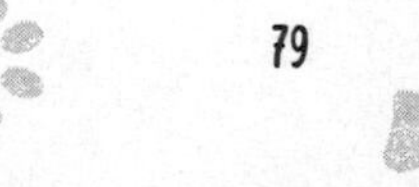

- Chestnut loves to run. He actually gallops, almost like a horse. "He once chased a deer through some fields," Brent says, "and he was beautiful to watch." Chestnut can run up to five miles. And he's always up for a hike with the family.

Grandfatherly Wisdom

"Having an older dog is just special," Brandi says. "It's like having this wise, old grandfather move into your house. And they're just so grateful. It's like they know, 'Oh, we've seen it bad, and this is good.' They're also more loyal. It's almost like they know that you chose them out of all the other dogs. Older dogs still have so much to give, and you don't have a lot of the puppy troubles. Just give them a chance, and they can blend right in."

"They're sweeter than you think," Jack says, "and they appreciate you more."

"They definitely have a lot left to give," says Brent. "Chestnut has given us way more than we've given him."

"If we had a farm," says Jack, "we'd take them all!"

POOH BEAR

MISS POOH BERRY PIE

Pooh Bear is the newest member of Barbara's Bear Gang. With a person of her own to love and four-legged friends to play with, Pooh Bear is so grateful to have found her forever home.

BREED: chow chow and Labrador retriever mix

AGE: about 12 years old

SIZE: 74 pounds

GENDER: female

POOH BEAR'S PERSON: Barbara Muncy

FUN FACT

Pooh Bear does the **sploot**. Not many big dogs do the sploot, but Pooh Bear will sploot just about anytime and anywhere. She even splooted in the middle of the mall while waiting to see Santa!

sploot: when a dog stretches out on its tummy with its front paws forward and its back legs spread out behind. A *sploot* means a dog feels perfectly happy and safe right where it is.

Only a Visit

Pooh Bear came to Old Friends from a rescue shelter in Georgia. Her owner had given her to the shelter when Hurricane Irma was about to hit, back in 2017. When the shelter filled up because of the coming storm, it moved some of its dogs to other shelters. By moving animals to other places, the shelter would be able to rescue even more dogs when the storm arrived. Old Friends stepped in to help and took several of the dogs. One of them was named Pooh.

Like many others, Barbara first found Old Friends on Facebook. She quickly fell in love with their mission and, of course, the dogs. In a word, she was hooked. She filled out an application, thinking, *If I find a dog I like, I'll be ready.* Old Friends, however, thought that meant she needed a dog right away—and that's how Barbara adopted the first of several old friends. His name was Jack.

Then, in 2017, Barbara saw Pooh on the Old Friends Facebook page. Pooh was a big, fuzzy black dog—which is the very best kind, if you ask Barbara. She brought Pooh home. *Only for a visit, though.* Well, that visit has stretched into a few years. Pooh stepped right into Barbara's home and heart, and she has been part of the family ever since.

And it makes perfect sense that Pooh belongs in Barbara's family of dogs. You see, Barbara has a tradition of giving all her dogs the middle name "Bear." So when Pooh came along and needed a home, Barbara just knew she'd fit right in as Pooh Bear. As for her nickname of "Miss Pooh Berry Pie," well, that's easy. Pooh Bear is as sweet as any pie!

The Bear Gang

Pooh Bear quickly made herself at home with the rest of Barbara's "Bear Gang." First, there's Bear Bear. His nickname is "Bee Boo," and he's a sixty-pound, fluffy black fellow. Bear Bear is a border collie mix with just a touch of German shepherd thrown in. He's been part of the Bear Gang since 2016 and is definitely the momma's boy of the bunch. One adorable thing about Bear Bear is that one ear is forever tilted up while the other is always flopped down. Bear Bear was bonded to Buddy, a smaller corgi mix. So, of course, Buddy Bear joined the family too!

Angel Bear is a sweet golden cocker spaniel. She was picked up as a stray. When no one claimed her, Old Friends stepped in to make sure she got a home. She joined the Bear Gang in 2017. And even though she has the sweet, sad, puppy-dog eyes of a cocker spaniel, Angel Bear is as happy as happy can be to live with Barbara and the rest of the gang.

Guard Dogs?

Pooh Bear and Bear Bear are dedicated guard dogs. Well, they're really good at guarding *one* door of the house anyway. You see, Barbara has a camera that lets her check in

on her furry friends while she's at work. That's how she knows that Pooh Bear and Bear Bear like to nap close to the door that leads to the garage. It's the very best spot because they can see Barbara as soon as she returns home.

However, the Bears haven't quite figured out that Barbara can come and go through other doors too. If a friend picks her up, Barbara will go out the front door. So naturally, she comes back in the house that way too. And where are Pooh Bear and Bear Bear? They're still sitting and waiting for her by the door to the garage!

What Is a Bonded Pair?

A **bonded pair** is two (or sometimes three) dogs who are strongly attached to one another. Bonded pairs will often eat, sleep, and play together. If they are separated, the dogs can get anxious or stressed.

It often takes longer for bonded pairs to be adopted. Most people only want to take one dog. Taking care of two dogs means twice the food, twice the bills, and twice the cleanup. But it can also mean twice the fun! Bonded pairs help each other adjust to their new home, and they keep one another—and you—entertained.

At the Old Friends Senior Dog Sanctuary, you'll find several bonded pairs, including Cinnamon and Oreo, a pair of bonded cocker spaniels.

Paper Beware!

Pooh Bear may not be the best guard dog, but if you ever need any papers shredded, she's the dog for the job. She *loves* to tear up and eat paper, cardboard, books, and magazines. Any paper or cardboard left out will surely be taste-tested. And because Barbara is an accountant, there's always plenty of paper around. "Pooh Bear has left her mark on quite a bit of my work," Barbara says.

Pooh Bear doesn't stop at paper either. She has also eaten a sock, an eye mask, and parts of some blankets. She even took a bite out of the Bible! Oh well. At least she has good taste.

Pooh Bear Goes to Church

Perhaps it was Pooh Bear's visits to church that tempted her to "taste" the Word of God. You see, Barbara's church sometimes has an outdoor service. On those days, Pooh Bear gets to join her for worship. She is a perfect lady in church and gets along with everyone she meets, whether they are two-legged or four-legged friends. Who knows? One day maybe they'll let her sing in the choir!

Pooh Bear also enjoys meeting up with all of her four-legged friends in the Best Friends Walking Club at church.

They stroll along a trail nearby. There's even a creek for them to splash in when the weather is warm. Pooh Bear will tell you, though, that playing in the water in front of strangers just isn't her thing. In fact, she won't even take a drink of water in front of people she doesn't know!

Pooh Bear is the only one of the Bear Gang who gets to go to church, but there are times when the whole gang goes for a ride. Getting all the dogs in the car at the same time can be quite a challenge! Pooh Bear always calls *shotgun!* so she can be Barbara's copilot. Fortunately the others are happy to spread out in the back.

Pawsome Facts About Pooh Bear

- Pooh Bear is super-fuzzy—she even has fuzzy toes! And she uses her extra-fuzzy eyebrows to say all kinds of things, like *Don't you think I need a treat now?* and *Wouldn't you just love to scratch behind my ears?*
- Belly rubs are Pooh Bear's absolute favorite, and she will roll over to show you her tummy. *Hint, hint!*
- If Pooh Bear could talk, she would say, *The best thing about morning walks is getting to chase the neighbor's cat.* Unfortunately (or maybe fortunately!), Pooh Bear is on a leash while the cat is not. And that rascally cat loves to dance just outside of Pooh Bear's reach.

Always Wagging

There's just something extra special about old friends. They're the kind of friends who are able to say *I love you* and *You're important to me*—without even saying a word. Old friends seem to know the value of things like simply sitting next to someone and being together. They understand that a hug or a good scratch on the ear is an excellent way to make any day better.

"Pooh Bear," Barbara says, "is one of the happiest pups I've ever seen. Her tail is always wagging." Pooh Bear and the rest of the gang have shown Barbara how important it is to look for ways to enjoy life and be happy. And, of course, never miss an opportunity to nap.

"Life is just better with dogs," Barbara says.

And the Bear Gang would all surely say, *Life is just better with Barbara.*

What Is a Chow Chow?

The chow chow, or chow, is known for the lion's mane of fur around its head and its blue-black tongue. Chows have been seen in Chinese art dating all the way back to 200 BC.

What Is a Labrador Retriever?

The Labrador retriever, or Lab, is one of the most popular dog breeds because it's so gentle, friendly, and loyal. It was first bred to swim out and retrieve ducks for hunters. The Lab's thick tail helps it steer as it swims. These beautiful dogs come in golden, black, and chocolate colors.

CHARLIE

THE SHADOW

When a short visit turns into a forever foster home, that's the recipe for a happily ever after!

BREED: cockapoo

AGE: about 13 years old

SIZE: 30 pounds

GENDER: male

CHARLIE'S PERSON: Noriko Ryan

FUN FACT

Charlie loves to chase tennis balls and his shadow. He catches the balls just fine, but he hasn't caught his shadow . . . yet.

A Place to Heal

When Old Friends found Charlie, he needed surgery for a hernia, which is a tear in one of the stomach muscles. Charlie's first owner was not able to pay for the surgery, so he was dropped off at a shelter. Because he was already about ten years old, it's likely that Charlie would have been put down in the shelter. Shelters have so many animals to care for that they just don't have the resources to help dogs like Charlie. Fortunately Old Friends found out about him. They picked him up and made sure he got the surgery he needed.

There was only one problem. After the surgery, Charlie would need a quiet place to recover for a few weeks. And even though the sanctuary is a wonderful place for dogs, it is not quiet! Charlie needed a foster home—and fast. That's when Noriko stepped in to help. She had been a volunteer with Old Friends since 2014, back when they were still in the original cabin. Noriko had already fostered a few senior dogs, so she agreed to take Charlie home with her for a month. The surgery was a complete success, and Charlie came to stay with Noriko while he healed.

When the month was up, Charlie went back to Old Friends to wait for a forever foster. But he had gotten used to the peace and quiet of Noriko's home. He wasn't happy with all of the noise and other dogs at the sanctuary. So Noriko took him back home with her—where he's lived happily ever since.

Charlie's one-month visit has stretched into years, and both he and Noriko are so glad to be forever friends.

WHAT IS A COCKAPOO?

A cockapoo is a dog that is a mix of cocker spaniel and poodle. Because they don't shed much, these dogs are often a great choice for people who suffer from allergies.

What Am I Going to Do with This Dog?

Charlie's happily ever after didn't quite start out that way. In fact, the first time Noriko saw him, Charlie had just come out of surgery. He'd been shaved. He was all groggy and droopy. And, well, let's just say he wasn't looking his best. Noriko took one look at him and thought, *He is so ugly! What am I going to do with this dog?* But of course, what she *did* was take him home and love and care for him.

Noriko laughs when she remembers that first meeting. "He grew on me though. Now Charlie is my buddy. He's my shadow."

At home Charlie follows Noriko everywhere she goes. He seems to know that she's his special friend. He lounges on the couch to watch TV with her and sleeps with her each night. When it's time for Noriko to head to work in the morning, he follows her downstairs and waits patiently by the door for her to come home. He may be an old man in doggy years, but Charlie will always be Noriko's baby.

Seven Dogs!

Noriko got started with fostering senior dogs when a friend told her about the Old Friends Senior Dog Sanctuary. She started following them on Facebook and got to know the

dogs they cared for. "I saw one dog," Noriko remembers, "and he had been on Facebook for so long. Nobody took him home, and I just felt so bad for him. I thought, *I'll take him*. That was my first old friend, and now I've had eleven old friends. Right now, I have seven.

"I remember this one time I went to a meeting of the fosters. This was when I was first getting started with senior dogs," Noriko says. "I met this lady who had seven dogs. I told my friend about it: 'Can you believe this lady has *seven* dogs?' And now look at me! *I have seven dogs!*"

It seems that collecting old friends can get to be a habit—and what a wonderful habit to have!

derp: when an animal's tongue hangs out of its mouth.

CHARLIE'S PACK OF PALS

Fortunately for other old friends, Noriko's heart has room for more than just one dog. Charlie now has six "fur" brothers and sisters—and most of them are old friends. Even though Charlie struggled with all the dogs at the sanctuary, he gets along just fine with his pals at Noriko's house.

- Lincoln Parker is the newest member of Noriko's pack. He's a sixteen-year-old Chihuahua. No one knows his history. Old Friends found him at a shelter, and Noriko took him home. Though he has no teeth, he has no trouble eating. And he seems to get along just fine as Noriko's second shadow—trotting along right after Charlie.
- Paisley is a shih tzu. When she first came home with Noriko, she struggled to walk. Old Friends helps her with special laser treatments and physical therapy. That, combined with Noriko's love and care, has made all the difference. Paisley can now go up and down steps by herself. She can even walk almost a quarter of a mile through the neighborhood, which is quite a long way for little legs!
- Paloma and Snow are a bonded pair of Chihuahuas. They are thirteen years old and have lost their teeth. That's why their tongues are always hanging out in the most adorable little derps. Even without teeth, they love their crunchy kibble. "They came to me so skinny," Noriko laughs, "but now they're a little on the chubby side." Let's just say they're well taken care of!
- Abigail and Darcie are both golden retrievers. Though they are not from Old Friends, they are both rescues. Darcie believes he is the king of the house, but he is happy to let the other dogs think they are in charge once in a while. Always smiling, Abigail is just thrilled to be part of the pack.

The Doctor Is In

While many old friends are as healthy as younger dogs, some of them do need extra care, like Charlie's hernia surgery. And most older dogs need some sort of regular medicine. All that can quickly add up to a lot of money—more money than many people can afford. That's what makes Old Friends such a blessing. They take care of all the dogs' medical care.

Old Friends can do this because they have their own vet, Dr. Christine. She makes sure every dog—those in the sanctuary and the ones in forever foster homes—gets a regular checkup and all the right vaccinations and medicines. Still, some dogs need extra care that Dr. Christine isn't able to provide in her small office at GrandPaw's Gardens. She works with veterinary specialists all around Nashville to make sure those dogs get whatever treatments they need. That might be X-rays for broken bones, surgeries, treatments for eye trouble or cancer, or even some physical therapy on an underwater treadmill! And it's all at no charge to the forever fosters.

"That's the only way I can keep all these dogs," Noriko says.

Old Friends is able to provide medical care for the dogs because of all the generous donations they receive. When people donate to Old Friends, it makes a big difference in the lives of these dogs. Those donations are also helping to build the new sanctuary, which will include a much bigger and better clinic for Dr. Christine. Once it opens, she'll be able to do X-rays and surgeries right there at the sanctuary.

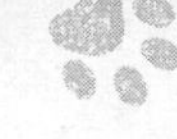

It's a Dog's Life!

The day starts pretty early for Charlie and his pals. First, it's time to *streeetch* and then take a trip outside. After that, it's time for breakfast and one more trip outside.

Before Noriko leaves for work, she turns on some music for the gang. "They seem to like jazz best," she says. "I've tried all different kinds of music, but they like jazz best." With the tunes playing, Noriko heads off to work, and Charlie settles down by the door to wait for her return.

Charlie and his pals are blessed with a wonderful friend who stops by around lunchtime to check on them. Then evening time rolls around, and Charlie's wait for Noriko is over at last! There's dinner to chow down and an evening of snuggling on the couch. At bedtime Charlie claims the best spot in the house—in bed right next to his favorite person.

On sunny days, Noriko takes all the dogs for a walk—all at the same time! "I load the smaller dogs into a buggy," she explains. "Charlie, Abigail, and Darcie are on their leashes." Then it's off they go for a trip around the neighborhood. The neighbors all know Charlie and his friends. Some of them even keep treats for the dogs—and the dogs all know exactly which neighbors have the treats!

PAWSOME FACTS ABOUT CHARLIE

- Charlie doesn't care a lot about toys . . . except tennis balls. He *loves* to chase tennis balls. And if they happen to be the kind that squeak when he catches them? Well, that's the very best kind!
- Charlie doesn't seem to know that he's a dog. He thinks he's just as human as Noriko. After all, he hangs out with her on the couch and sleeps on the bed. Now, if he can just convince her to let him eat off the table . . .

SPLASHING THROUGH THE WAVES

One of Noriko's favorite times with Charlie was at the beach. A couple of years ago, they took a trip down to Port St. Joe in Florida. It was Charlie's first time to take such a long ride in the car, but he loved every minute!

The beach brought out the puppy in Charlie. It didn't matter how cold the weather was, he would trot up and down the beach, sniffing and checking everything out. Charlie quickly discovered that splashing through the waves to chase a tennis ball is *so much* better than chasing one through the grass at home.

Good Company

When Noriko first began fostering older dogs, she was surprised by how active they were. Now she loves to see how fun and playful each one can be. "And they are just so much company," she says.

"So many people look at the puppies," Noriko continues. "I know the puppies are cute, but these older dogs are so cute too. I wish more kids would take the older dogs. Even though these guys are old, they can still learn. They can still play. We've got to rescue as many of the older dogs from the shelters as we can."

Because every dog deserves a happily ever after . . . just like Charlie.

HUDSON BROWN

A DAPPER DOG

Who's the super-cool dog with the spiffy bow tie? Why, that's old Hudson Brown—the most dapper dog around!

BREED: chocolate Labrador mix

AGE: about 16 years old

SIZE: 70 pounds

GENDER: male

HUDSON BROWN'S PEOPLE: Cindy and Rob Porter

FUN FACT

At eight thirty every night, Hudson Brown knows it's time for bedtime cookies. He will come up to Cindy or Rob and push on their hands or whimper just a little. *Hey,* he seems to say, *don't forget it's cookie time!*

A New Life for Old Hudson Brown

Just a few years ago, the Porters were content with their two dogs and a cat. But when they lost one of those dogs, the dog who was left behind—twelve-year-old Colby Jack—was sick with sadness and loneliness. Cindy and Rob thought a new friend might be just the thing to cheer him up. That's when they turned to Old Friends Senior Dog Sanctuary.

Cindy first found Old Friends when she drove past GrandPaw's Gardens one day. Curious, she decided to check them out on Facebook. When she did, she was amazed by what she found. "They had so many followers—all because they decided to do this beautiful thing of taking in some old dogs no one else wanted," she says. Cindy reached out to the sanctuary and said she was looking for a larger, laid-back kind of dog who would let Colby be in charge. That's how they came to meet Hudson.

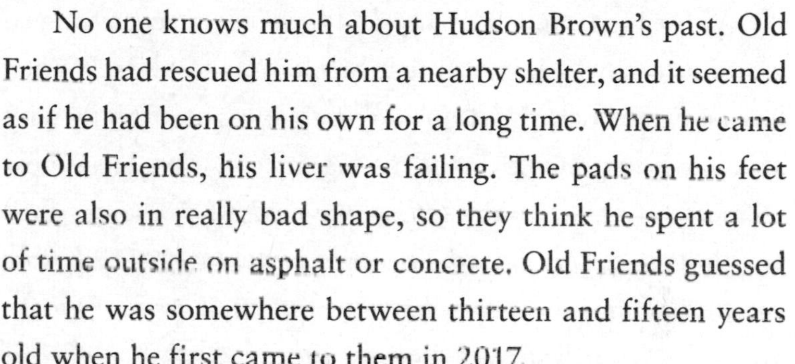

No one knows much about Hudson Brown's past. Old Friends had rescued him from a nearby shelter, and it seemed as if he had been on his own for a long time. When he came to Old Friends, his liver was failing. The pads on his feet were also in really bad shape, so they think he spent a lot of time outside on asphalt or concrete. Old Friends guessed that he was somewhere between thirteen and fifteen years old when he first came to them in 2017.

Before Hudson could come home with the Porters, they needed to make sure he could get along with Colby. So Cindy and Rob took Colby to the sanctuary to meet Hudson because it was neutral ground—not Colby's own home turf. When the two dogs met, Colby strutted all around, trying to prove he was in charge. But that didn't bother Hudson at all. So after they were approved, the Porters brought him home.

What did Colby think of his new fur-brother? At first Colby gave Cindy and Rob a big dose of the stink eye. But the truth is, Hudson Brown really brought Colby back to life and helped him get over the sadness of losing his friend.

Colby wasn't the only one Hudson had to get used to though. There was also the cat, Tessie. She was a fourteen-year-old terror who *hated* dogs. In fact, she liked to pretend there weren't even any dogs in her house. At least until Hudson Brown came along. Though Tessie is gone now, there were times when she would actually snuggle up with Hudson. Oh, she never stopped hating dogs, but that big brown one? He was okay.

As for Hudson, Cindy says, "I have never seen a dog so grateful to have a home. It just brought us to tears." When he first came home, Hudson stared up at his new family with absolute love pouring out of his big, brown eyes. He almost seemed to say, *So you're telling me that all I have to do is get along with this grouchy brother and a hissy, dog-hating cat, and I can live indoors, have my own bed, regular meals,* and *a cookie at bedtime? Sign me up!*

In addition to Hudson's big, brown eyes, he has the most adorable **snoot**. It's perfect for **booping**!

snoot: an adorable dog nose

boop: to playfully tap a snoot

Hudson Brown: Ace Reporter

The only thing the Porters know for certain about Hudson Brown's past is his name. That's because when he was picked up, he was wearing a name tag that said "Hudson." So where did the "Brown" come from?

Cindy laughs and says, "We've always given our dogs two names because we're southern. Hudson is a chocolate Lab, so 'Brown' just seemed to fit. We think Hudson Brown sounds like he could have been a reporter from the 1950s. I can just see him wearing one of those fedora hats with a pencil tucked behind his ear. We've made up so many funny stories about an imaginary past life for him. And Hudson just looks at us like, *Yeah whatever, Mom and Dad. Just give me a cookie.*"

Trouble to the Max

In 2018, about a year after the Porters got Hudson, Cindy spotted Max on a collie rescue site. He was also a senior dog, about ten years old at the time. Max was just so beautiful, so she asked Rob, "Do you think we could handle another dog?"

Colby and Hudson were such good, well-behaved dogs that Rob said, "Yeah, sure. We've got two of the best dogs in the world—what's one more?"

And then they got Max.

Have your parents ever warned you about friends who might tempt you to do the wrong things? Well, Max is that friend. He gets sweet Hudson into *all kinds* of trouble.

For instance, when Hudson first came to live with Cindy and Rob, he didn't bark at all. In fact, they thought he couldn't bark, that maybe his voice had been injured at some point. But then Max came and taught Hudson how to bark. Now Hudson barks at *everything*. Thanks, Max.

One especially funny time that Max dragged Hudson into trouble was actually the night that Tessie the cat died. Cindy and Rob were out in the backyard, giving her a proper funeral. At the same time, their new neighbors were moving into the house right next door. (Don't you wonder what they thought about those people with the shovel burying something in their backyard?) Cindy and Rob think they must have forgotten to close the backyard gate that night. Because the next evening when Cindy came home from work, she spotted Hudson lying in the neighbor's yard with a bowl of water next to him. Max and Colby were in the backyard with the gate closed. So what on earth was Hudson doing outside the gate?

When Cindy went inside the house, a phone message was waiting from her neighbors. When she called them, they laughed and explained: "We just turned around and there was this big collie [Max] inside our house. We checked his tag and saw your address and phone number. We put him in the backyard and closed the gate. The big Lab [Hudson] was just lying outside, but he wouldn't let us

put him back inside the fence. So we gave him some water and called you."

Cindy believes that this is what happened: When Max saw that the gate was open, he double-dog dared Hudson to go outside. She can just hear him saying something like, *Come on! They left the gate open. Let's go!* Then Max—who hates to be outside for long—trotted right over to the neighbors' house and just went inside. Poor rule-following Hudson was probably scared to death. He knew he wasn't supposed to be outside the gate, and he knew he shouldn't just go waltzing into some strangers' house. He probably thought, *Uh-oh! I'm in so much trouble. I'm just going to lie right here and not make it any worse!*

Oh, Max.

It's a Bird, It's a Plane, It's . . . Hudson Brown!

Did you know dogs can fly? Well, Hudson Brown can! His fur-brother Colby has this habit of lying in doorways or on the steps of the stairway. Because Hudson is such a dapper gentleman—and because he's just a little bit afraid of Colby—he doesn't try to move Colby. He doesn't seem to want to risk upsetting his sometimes-grouchy big brother. He doesn't even bark or make any sound at all. Instead, Hudson Brown crouches down and leaps, flying right over him as if he has wings. Even on the stairs! He's like Superman leaping over sleeping dogs in a single bound.

That's not the only time Hudson Brown's gentlemanly side comes out. Every day the Porters take the dogs for a walk around the neighborhood. But they only take two of them at a time. When Hudson walks with Colby, he takes it slow and easy, just the way Colby likes. But when he walks with Max—who likes to move fast—Hudson picks up his speed to stay right by his side. "Hudson is so easygoing," Cindy says. "He just changes to fit to whatever Colby or Max needs."

A People Pup

Though Hudson enjoys walking and hanging out with his four-legged fur-brothers, he's definitely a people person . . . *um*, pup. He wants to be wherever his people are, and he definitely misses them when they're gone.

Hudson even knows when it's time for Rob to get home from work. He'll stand in front of the door that leads into the garage, lay his head against it, and wait for Rob to come in. And if Cindy is working in the kitchen, he's sure to keep an eye on her—and be ready to help with cleanup duty if any bits of food happen to fall.

Even when he's sleeping, he wants to be with his people. Hudson will nap in whatever room Cindy and Rob are in. And at nighttime, his bed is right next to theirs.

Destroy the Squeaker!

The Porters will tell you that Hudson Brown is one of the calmest dogs around. Except when it comes to squeakers.

The Porters don't believe Hudson ever really had toys before he came to live with them. Now he has all the toys a dog could want. He loves his stuffed toys, especially the ones with squeakers. Or rather, he loves *destroying* the toys with squeakers. He tosses them in the air and chases after them. When he hits the squeaker, he goes crazy. He bounces around and seems to shout, *I've got to get that squeaker! I've got to get that squeaker!* Hudson will chew and shred and gnaw on that toy until he gets the squeaker out. Fortunately his toys are the only thing Hudson chews and destroys!

Pawsome Facts About Hudson Brown

- Hudson's nicknames are "Hershey Kiss" and "Frosted Chocolate Cupcake."
- He has the most amazing eyebrows. Hudson can have whole conversations by just waggling his eyebrows at you.
- Even though Max was a senior dog when he came to live with them, he had been an outside dog and wasn't house-trained. Hudson quickly took care of that, teaching him when and where to do his business outside.

- Hudson loves to have his ears scratched. And he makes the funniest noises when you hit just the right spot.

You know that old saying that you can't teach an old dog new tricks? It's totally false. They learn all the time. "Hudson learned our routines," Cindy says. "He knows when we come and go. Every morning, he comes and stands by the bed to get his medicine—which is wrapped inside a yummy pill pocket. And he definitely knows when it's time for bedtime cookies."

These senior dogs are pretty good at showing their people a few new tricks too. Like how to be grateful for a second chance. And how love changes lives—whether you've got four legs or only two.

JUNEBUG

THE SWEETEST OLD FRIEND AROUND

Some dogs are flashy and win Best in Show. Some dogs are super-talented and do all kinds of tricks. But JuneBug has them all beat—she's simply the sweetest old friend around.

BREED: Chihuahua, terrier, and corgi mix

AGE: between 11 and 13 years old

SIZE: about 10 pounds

GENDER: female

JUNEBUG'S PEOPLE: Kelly, Daniel, Reece, and Preston Williams

FUN FACT

Instead of barking like most dogs do, JuneBug makes a sharp little *chirp!* sound. It's kind of like a bird dog. Or maybe it's a dog bird. Nah! It's just JuneBug!

Love at First Sight

JuneBug was rescued from a **hoarding** situation in 2017 and taken to a nearby animal shelter. Old Friends found her there and brought her to the sanctuary. The vet checked her out and guessed that she was about ten years old at that time. This sweet little girl only stayed at the sanctuary for about three weeks, though, before she was scooped up by the Williams family.

JuneBug's new beginning started in a most unusual way: with Daniel's fear of big dogs. You see, Kelly and Daniel decided to get a second dog for their family. They

already had a cockapoo named Ruger. Ruger was a bit hyper and anxious, so the Williams family needed to be careful to get a dog he could get along with. They first went to the local shelter. That's where Daniel fell in love with a beautiful big dog, and they took him home. But no one had any idea that Daniel had a hidden fear of big dogs.

As a child, Daniel had once been chased up onto the roof of a car by his neighbor's large dogs. Though he had mostly forgotten all about it, when the family brought that big dog home from the shelter, all the anxiety and fear of that day came rushing back. Then, when the new dog acted a little strange around their thirteen-year-old son Preston and later growled at its own reflection in the window, Daniel's fears only got worse. He and Kelly realized they didn't have any experience with big dogs. In their heads, they knew the dog would probably be fine with a little time. But in their hearts, they also knew they were just not a big dog family. With heavy hearts, they returned the dog to the shelter.

Kelly and Daniel still wanted another dog for their family. Just not a big dog. However, since they had returned a dog—even though they had him for only three days—they could not get another shelter dog. Then one day, Kelly drove by the Old Friends Senior Dog Sanctuary. She wondered, *What is this place?* So she stopped in to see what they were about.

Old Friends to the Rescue!

"The staff at Old Friends was ridiculously kind," Kelly says. "I just walked in and I told them, 'I have a question. Before I fill out an application, you need to know that I returned a dog to the shelter. Also, I already have a dog who's very hyper and a bit anxious. We can't have any big dogs, and my house has stairs. But we'd really like to get another dog. Is it worth it to fill out an application, or is our situation too much trouble?'"

"Absolutely!" the Old Friends worker answered. "We've got lots of dogs, and we can find one that will fit with your family."

Kelly filled out the application, and Old Friends came out to check her home. Based on her family's needs, the staff at Old Friends chose four dogs for them to meet. These were dogs they thought would fit in well with Ruger and Kelly and her family. The whole family went to the sanctuary to meet the dogs.

The One

So how did Kelly know JuneBug was the one for her family? "Well," she laughs, "I didn't." In fact, when Kelly first saw JuneBug's pictures on Facebook, she secretly hoped JuneBug wasn't one of the dogs the staff would pick for them. You see, JuneBug is an absolutely beautiful dog—on the inside. And once you get to know and love her, she's beautiful on the outside too. But when people first meet her . . . well, her beauty is not the first thing anyone notices. In fact, she has a mohawk. There's a patch of hair right on top of her head that sticks straight up!

When Kelly and her family arrived at Old Friends to meet the four dogs the staff had selected, guess who was one of the four dogs? JuneBug! *Oh well*, Kelly thought, *that's okay. My family will pick one of the other three.*

But guess what? They didn't. They picked JuneBug.

Now Kelly knows that JuneBug was the best choice they could have ever made. She gets along wonderfully with hyper Ruger. Sometimes he will growl at her, and she'll just sass him right back—even though she's less than half his size! JuneBug never fights with him, but she stands her ground and doesn't let him bully her either.

In fact, JuneBug has helped calm Ruger down. They'll often lie on the living room rug together, each with their own bone, happily chewing away. That's a quiet scene that Kelly thought would never happen! JuneBug is calm and chill—and she's teaching Ruger how to be calm and chill too.

Except when it comes to food . . .

JuneBug's Favorite Things

JuneBug doesn't just like food, she *adores* it. And she knows when it's time to eat. About thirty minutes or so before

feeding time, she'll go over to her bowl and *chirp*—just to make sure no one forgets that it's time to eat!

What does JuneBug enjoy eating? Everything—new foods, old foods, treats, table foods, even carrots. JuneBug eats it all. Except strawberries. She hates strawberries.

Next to eating, JuneBug's most loved thing to do is play. Fetch is one of her most favorite games. Whether it's with a stuffed animal or a ball, she is amazing at fetch and will play it for half an hour or more.

JuneBug's other favorite game is hide-and-seek. Kelly works from home, and JuneBug likes to keep an eye on her. "But sometimes," Kelly says, "I'll get up to get a drink of water, and she'll lose sight of me. She'll circle all around the house looking for me, and I'll play hide-and-seek with her, ducking all around to stay out of sight." JuneBug's pretty hard to beat at this game though. Sooner or later, she always finds Kelly—no matter where she tries to hide.

And Then Came Leonard

Leonard is the newest member of the Williams family. He's an adorable little Chihuahua mix who is also from Old Friends. He's been with the family only a few months, but he fits right in.

Like most rescues, not much is known about Leonard's

history. Old Friends believes he's somewhere between eight and twelve years old. And sadly, they also think that at some point, someone was not very nice to Leonard. In the beginning, he was so frightened of people that he would pee as soon as he was picked up. He doesn't do that anymore, now that he's safe and loved in his forever home with the Williams family.

Unlike JuneBug, Leonard doesn't play very much—he doesn't seem to know how. But he does love chewing on bones, and his new family makes sure he has plenty to enjoy. While JuneBug is definitely little brother Preston's dog, it's eighteen-year-old Reece whom Leonard loves best.

Perhaps the most adorable thing about Leonard is the way he begs. He stands up on his hind legs and taps the tips of his front paws together—exactly like he's saying, *more, more!* in sign language.

A Bed for Every Dog and a Dog for Every Bed

When it comes to napping, JuneBug loves dog beds. And there are several scattered all around that are perfect for taking a little snooze in. You might also find JuneBug, Ruger, and Leonard catching a little nap on the couch or one of the pillows.

At dinnertime JuneBug likes to lie in a dog bed next to the dining table. While Ruger and Leonard are usually begging at the table, JuneBug waits patiently nearby, seeming to say, *I know you'll take care of me*. Of course, each of the dogs can count on getting a tasty little bite or two.

When bedtime rolls around, there's a dog for every bed. Ruger sleeps with Kelly and Daniel, Leonard sleeps with Reece, and JuneBug sleeps with Preston—just as she has since the first day she came to live with the family.

In fact, JuneBug has her own special little bedtime routine. After a quick trip outside, she runs upstairs with Preston to his room. Because she's a little thing, she first hops up on a little stair and then onto an ottoman. Next she jumps from the ottoman to the bed. Then she trots up to her pillow. (It's a double bed, so there are two pillows—one for Preston and one for JuneBug.) After a quick circle around, JuneBug settles down for the night.

Pawsome Facts About JuneBug

- JuneBug is a nose nudger. That is, if someone is on the couch, she'll jump up next to them and nudge them with her nose to be petted. She *loves* to be petted.
- According to JuneBug, trips in the car are so much fun. JuneBug also enjoys walking, but only for short walks. And of course, she has to stop to smell everything along the way.
- Some of the stairs in JuneBug's home are covered with

carpet, but the last few stairs at the bottom are wood. Because she once slipped on those wooden stairs, she doesn't like to walk down them anymore. So she just sits on the last carpeted step and *chirps* until someone comes. Don't pick her up though! JuneBug is scared of heights. To help her down the stairs, Kelly holds her hand under JuneBug's head—it's enough to let JuneBug know she won't let her fall.

- You probably already know this, but the vacuum cleaner is evil. Don't worry though. JuneBug will bark loud and long to warn you that it's coming.

The Dream Life

Neither JuneBug nor Leonard had a great start in life. But with the Williams family, they have found the life dogs dream of. Fear and hunger and cruelty are all things of the past. When tummies rumble, a little *chirp* or a bark brings food. When it's time for fun, there are games of fetch and hide-and-seek to play. And when bedtime rolls around, each dog has its own special place to lay its head.

JuneBug and Leonard—and Ruger too—are surrounded by love and plenty of tail-wagging goodness, which is just the way it should be. In return, they give their humans all the love they have to give . . . which, as it turns out, is quite a lot.

What Is a Chihuahua?

The tiny Chihuahua was the original purse dog. It only grows to be about five to eight inches tall and usually weighs less than six pounds. Its name comes from the Mexican state of Chihuahua, where these dogs were first discovered.

What Is a Corgi?

Corgis are low-to-the-ground dogs that were first bred to be cattle dogs. They are usually less than a foot tall, which allows them to nip at a cow's legs to get them headed in the right direction. *Corgi* comes from "kergie," which is Celtic for *dog*.

What Is a Terrier?

Terriers are a group of dogs known for being feisty, full of energy, and a bit stubborn. They were originally bred to hunt and kill small animals like rodents. Terriers come in a variety of sizes from the fifteen- to twenty-pound "Westie" all the way up to the fifty- to seventy-pound Airedale.

LANA

A HAPPY GIRL

When Sandi first saw Lana, she thought, *That's the saddest face I've ever seen.* But these days, you couldn't find a happier girl!

Meet Lana

BREED: mastiff

AGE: between 8 and 9 years old

SIZE: 135 pounds

GENDER: female

LANA'S PERSON: Sandi Chadwick

FUN FACT

The staff at Old Friends pronounced Lana's name as *Lah-na*. But Sandi quickly "southernized" her new friend's name to *Lan-na*.

Saving Lana

Lana came to Old Friends as a rescue from a local shelter. Though all the details of her history aren't known, her past was not a good one. The vet could tell that Lana had given birth to a lot of puppies. That means she was probably used for breeding in a puppy mill (like Lucy-Lu). Lana also hates closed-in spaces, so she was likely kept in a crate or a cage most of the time. Her tail was **docked**, or shortened, at some point. Since this isn't usually done to a mastiff, the vet believed her tail was injured—probably from scraping against the sides of a too-small cage for far too long. When Lana came to Old Friends, she weighed only 75 pounds—a healthy female mastiff should weigh somewhere between 120 and 170 pounds. Every one of her ribs was showing, and the vet feared she might not make it. Lana had a long way to go.

That's when Sandi came along.

Sandi wasn't looking for another dog. She already had old friends of her own at home. But one day, she stopped by the sanctuary to pick up some things for her dogs, and the staff said, "We have someone we want you to meet." They knew Sandi had a special place in her heart for bigger dogs. At that point, Lana was still back in the medical part of the sanctuary. They were feeding her three meals a day to try to put some weight back on her.

The first time Sandi saw Lana, she remembers thinking, *That's the saddest face I've ever seen.* It was as if Lana seemed to be saying, *I don't know where I am or why I am here, but these people are feeding me.* When asked what convinced her that Lana belonged at home with her, Sandi says, "It was her eyes. She watched everything." Lana may not have been able to follow Sandi and the staff around the medical room that day, but her eyes followed them everywhere. "She wanted to see and know everything that was going on. And I like big dogs," Sandi says with a smile. "I know it's harder to find fosters for big dogs. They can be expensive to feed." (Right now, Lana eats about thirty-five pounds of kibble a month.) Sandi agreed to take her home as soon as she was ready.

But first, Lana needed to stay at the sanctuary a few more weeks to heal.

Finally, in December 2018, Lana was ready to go home. One of the Old Friends workers brought her to Sandi's house. For about an hour, Lana paced all around the house, sniffing and checking out everything. Then she picked out a spot, lay down, and slept for hours.

Lana was home.

What Is a Mastiff?

Mastiffs have been around for thousands of years. They are known for their huge, wrinkled heads that give them the look of being very wise and kind. In medieval times, mastiffs were used for hunting, guarding great estates, and even fighting in wars. Even William Shakespeare wrote about these wonderful dogs. Today's mastiffs are friendlier than their ancestors, but they are just as brave. These gentle giants make loving pets and are very protective of their families.

Lana Makes Four

Lana is Sandi's fifth forever foster. Sandi has three fosters living with her now—Lana, a blind basset hound named Henry, and a beagle named Sonny, who is also blind.

All dogs on deck! Several old friends line up to enjoy the fresh air.

There are lots of comfy spots to hang out with your dog pals at Old Friends.

Cinnamon and Oreo doing their favorite thing—cuddling with each other.

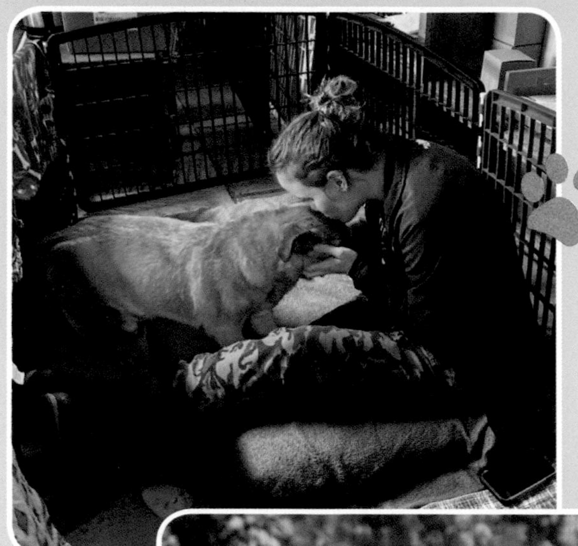

Staff member Marina loves on Brownie.

FreddieMac and Rosebud enjoy a sunny day at Old Friends.

The cubbies at Old Friends are supposed to hold supplies. But you'll usually find a dog or two enjoying the extra blankets.

Michael receives a warm welcome after being out of town for a few days.

Barry and Hobo like to sing.

Michael, Zina, and Old Friends workers celebrate the groundbreaking at the construction site of the new Old Friends building.

Lucy-Lu was the golden retriever who inspired Michael and Zina to start Old Friends Senior Dog Sanctuary.

Lucy-Lu (center) plays tug-of-war with two other goldies, Gracie (left) and Ginger (right). Michael and Zina kept several rescued dogs in their home before they started Old Friends.

Lucy-Lu usually had a chewing bone close by.

Leo's big personality helped Michael and Zina get the support they needed to start Old Friends.

Each summer, Leo got a "lion" cut to keep him cool in the Tennessee heat.

Maverick arrived at Old Friends after losing his owner.

Maverick's favorite spot to relax is the foot of John and Melinda's bed. PHOTO BY JOHN KNOTT III.

After getting Maverick settled, the Knotts returned to Old Friends for Maisy.

Maisy is so happy to be home!
PHOTO BY MELINDA KNOTT.

Old Friends volunteers take dogs for walks at a nearby park. Marco takes a break from his walk to get pet.

Marco is now calm and gentle in his new home with Robert.

Buddy was a big dog with a big voice! PHOTO BY KAY NORMAN.

Chestnut keeps an eye on soccer practice. He lets Coach know whenever practice runs late. PHOTO BY BRANDI FRUIN.

Chestnut and Sadie love to hang out. PHOTO BY BRANDI FRUIN.

Pooh Bear is just so fluffy! © PENNY ADAMS PHOTOGRAPHY. USED BY PERMISSION.

Barbara and Angel Bear share a cuddle. © JANE SOBEL KLONSKY. USED BY PERMISSION.

Charlie's favorite toys are tennis balls.
PHOTO BY NORIKO RYAN.

Charlie loved the wind and waves during a vacation in Florida.
PHOTO BY NORIKO RYAN.

Noriko wants to help rescue as many senior dogs as she can. She added Lincoln Parker to her pack in 2020.

Hudson Brown's muzzle has turned gray with age, but he's still as sweet as chocolate! PHOTOS BY CINDY PORTER.

The only thing anyone knows about Hudson Brown's past is his name. He wore this tag when he was found.

JuneBug was so happy to be safe when she came to Old Friends.

JuneBug loves her boy, Preston. JuneBug even has her own pillow on Preston's bed.
PHOTO BY KELLY WILLIAMS.

With Ruger, Leonard, and JuneBug, the Williamses are one big happy family!
PHOTO BY KELLY WILLIAMS.

At home with Sandi, every day is a good day for Lana.

At over 100 pounds, Shaq is a giant dog. And he is filled to the tip-top with sweetness. PHOTO BY RITA JAKES.

Shaq loves swimming in the lake in his backyard. PHOTO BY RITA JAKES.

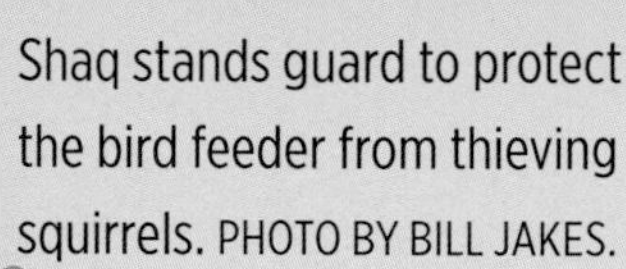

Shaq stands guard to protect the bird feeder from thieving squirrels. PHOTO BY BILL JAKES.

Prince doesn't let much bother him, including his blindness.

Prince is so handsome when he dresses up. PHOTO BY CUSTOM KARE KENNEL.

Over the years, Sally has brought home twenty-eight old friends, but Wally is an extra-special companion. PHOTO BY SALLY J. MCCANNER.

Zelda was supposed to stay at Jenny's house for only a couple weeks. But Jenny fell in love with sweet and sassy "Zelly" and just had to keep her. PHOTO BY JENNY CRUISE.

Zelda and Callahan are happy to live together—as long as Callahan doesn't try to take Zelda's spot on the couch. PHOTO BY JENNY CRUISE.

Mack knows his way around every corner of Old Friends, especially the locations of all the cozy cubbies.

When Mason works at his desk, Mack is very helpful.

Mack didn't like car rides at first. But just click his leash now, and he's ready to roll!

Mack competes in the 2020 Dog Bowl.

Mack gets all dressed up for his presidential campaign.

Mason and Nell became Mack's forever fosters in 2020.

Mack shows off during the *Homecoming Tales* cover photo shoot.

Although not a foster, a fourth dog also shares Lana's new home: Subito, a beagle. Even though she's much bigger than the others, Lana gets along great with all her fur-siblings. Sometimes she and Henry even curl up together for a nap—not *quite* touching, but sharing the same space.

Lana is very protective of her new family and home. The mastiff breed in general is very protective, but Lana is more so, especially around men. This may be because she is remembering a man in her past who was not kind to her. If one of the guys from Old Friends comes by, Lana remembers him and is fine. But with other men, it can take her a while to warm up to them. Like Sandi's son.

Lana Makes a New Friend

Sandi travels for work sometimes, so she has a dog sitter come to stay with her "babies." Because Lana struggles with meeting new people, the sitter spent a lot of time with her so Lana would be comfortable with her.

One Sunday night, just as Sandi was getting ready to leave town the next morning, the sitter called. She was in the hospital and couldn't come take care of the dogs. Sandi was desperate, so she called her son (who's all grown up). "Can you please come?" she asked. "I'll make sure you have plenty of treats to bribe Lana, and I'll get back as fast as I can." Thankfully he agreed. Sandi's son had met Lana before, but Lana still hadn't completely decided whether she liked him yet.

Sandi put up a baby gate to keep Lana in the kitchen, while Sandi's son stayed in the living room. Monday evening, he texted Sandi a message: *I'm having to toss treats to the far side of the kitchen to get to the refrigerator. She keeps trying to bite my feet.* Sandi texted back, *Well, she doesn't have any teeth, but wear your shoes just in case.*

When Sandi didn't hear back from her son, she started to worry. Then the next day, he sent her a picture of Lana lying at his feet, with toys all around them. It was as if Lana were saying, *Okay, here's the deal: I'll bring you all my toys, and you'll give me treats.*

Betty Crocker Beware!

Lana really enjoys her food—probably because she didn't have nearly enough to eat for far too long. In fact, when she first came to Sandi, Lana would eat anything and everything—and that doesn't just mean every kind of food. After she finished off the food in her bowl, Lana would try to eat the bowl itself! Maybe she was hoping more food would suddenly appear.

You might think that when a dog is so underweight, like Lana was, she should be fed as much as she wants and as often as she wants. But putting on weight too fast can be

unhealthy for a dog too. The vet wanted Lana to gain her weight back gradually, so Sandi kept a close eye on how much Lana ate—and *what* she ate.

That's because Lana didn't stop with eating food and bowls. She also ate paper, cardboard, and even rocks. That first Christmas, Sandi had to explain to her nephew why the box was missing from his Christmas present!

But the funniest thing Lana ever ate was Betty Crocker. Not a person, but a cookbook. When Sandi came home one afternoon, she found pages scattered all over her kitchen. And in the middle of it all lay her *Betty Crocker's Cookbook* cover with a giant bite taken out of it. Apparently all those pictures of delicious-looking food were too much for Lana to resist.

When Lana came to live with Sandi, her weight was up to about eighty pounds. It took six months of her eating three meals a day to get back to a healthy weight. Now she's down to two meals a day, which is what most dogs eat. And she's actually on a bit of a diet because Sandi did too good a job of putting weight on her! But at least Lana no longer snacks on bowls . . . or Betty Crocker.

WHATCHA GOT DOWN THERE?

As much as she loves her food, for the longest time Lana refused to go to the basement where all the dogs' food is kept. Every day Lana would watch Sandi go downstairs with empty food bowls. And then Lana would watch Sandi come back up again with bowls filled with wonderful food. Sandi says, "You could just see her thinking, *What kind of place is that down there?*"

Even though all of the other dogs went down into the basement—and came safely right back up again—Lana wouldn't give it a try. Maybe it reminded her of her past life in the cage. It was a little dark, and the stairs were narrow. Who knew what was down there? So whenever Sandi went downstairs, Lana would wait at the top of the steps and refuse to budge.

"One day," Sandi says, "I was down in the basement, and I felt this nudge on the back of my legs. It scared the life out of me! It was Lana." She couldn't stand the curiosity any longer. She just had to find out what was happening down in that basement and how those empty food bowls would suddenly be filled with food. Now Lana takes regular trips down the stairs to help Sandi fill the bowls. And maybe sneak a kibble or two.

The Escape Artist

One of the first things Lana figured out after moving into Sandi's house was how to escape her backyard fence. It wasn't that Lana wanted to run away though. Sandi would find her simply sitting on the other side of the fence. It was as if she just wanted to see if the grass really was greener on the other side.

At first Sandi was afraid Lana was jumping over the fence. After all, she's a big dog! But after a few days of watching her, Sandi figured out that Lana was using her massive head to push out the bottom of the chain-link fence. A quick trip to the hardware store put an end to Lana's escape artist days.

You might think a big dog like Lana would want lots of exercise and playtime, but she's a pretty low-energy dog. She enjoys a walk of about a half mile or so, and then she's ready to come back home.

Once in a while, Lana will try to play with the other dogs. But because Lana probably never had much chance to play as a puppy, she doesn't really know how. Also, she's kind of clumsy and tends to crash into things—which can be a little scary for the smaller dogs!

Lana does enjoy her toys though, especially her big, blue bone. She'll chew on it for hours. She also loves anything that squeaks, at least until she chews out the squeaker. And those flat squirrel toys without any stuffing? Those are the best! Once in a while, when she's feeling extra playful, Lana will roll around on her back, wiggling and wriggling just like a puppy—a gigantic, 135-pound puppy!

blep: when a dog's—or other animal's—
tongue is just barely poking out

PAWSOME FACTS ABOUT LANA

- When Lana sleeps, her tongue—usually just the tip—falls out. Dog lovers call that a **blep**.
- During the day, while Sandi is at work, Lana naps on a big dog bed near the back door. A window is there where she can watch for her favorite person to come home. At night her favorite spot to sleep is on the couch—the *whole* couch, of course.
- Every day, Lana, Henry, and Sonny have an ongoing "conversation" with the little Chihuahua next door. Of course, the Chihuahua is always the one who starts it, but their conversations are absolute noisy chaos!

TODAY IS A GOOD DAY

Lana lived through some of the worst times you could ever imagine. She almost didn't make it. But finding a new home with Sandi gave her a whole new chance to live her best life—a tail-wagging kind of life.

TIPS FOR MEETING BIG DOGS

Meeting a big dog can be scary at first because . . . well, they're big! In fact, when Lana stands on all fours, she is as tall as Sandi's five-year-old niece.

The first time you meet a big dog (or any dog), it's important to let the dog set the pace. Always ask the owner's permission to meet the dog, and do whatever they say. Each dog has its own personality and way it likes to be petted.

Even when the owner says it's okay, don't rush to pet a dog. Take it slow, and speak softly. Use the dog's name. Start with small pets. If the dog likes that, you can pet them more and maybe even work up to a big hug. No matter how big or how tiny a dog is, always be gentle.

If a dog wags its tail, lifts its head to you, or takes a friendly step toward you, it's probably okay to pet—with the owner's permission, of course. But if a dog growls or barks, tucks its tail, or curls its lips to show its teeth, back away slowly. It might not be ready to meet you yet.

"Just look at Lana," Sandi now says. "Look at that face. She's always smiling. Look how far she's come. She's such a happy girl. She loves living in a house, having her own backyard, and being part of a family. She's just so grateful still. To this day, every bowl of food is met with joy and dancing."

Lana doesn't worry about what happened in the past, and she doesn't worry about what might happen in the future. She lives in *this* moment, *today.* When it comes to her rescue dogs, Sandi says, "You give them the love and the home you wish they'd always had, and that's what they remember—what they have right now."

SHAQ

THE GENTLE GIANT

The first time you see Shaq, you just might think twice about saying hello. He's big. *Really big!* And his bark is even bigger. But don't let this massive guy—or his booming bark—fool you. Shaq is really a gentle giant.

BREED: Newfoundland and Labrador retriever mix

AGE: about 8 years old

SIZE: 107 pounds

GENDER: male

SHAQ'S PEOPLE: Rita and Bill Jakes

FUN FACT

Shaq loves to sit in chairs. If a chair is in the room, you're likely to find Shaq perched in it.

We've Got Your Dog

Shaq first came to live with his humans, Rita and Bill, on February 10, 2018. Before that, he had a bit of a rough time. Shaq was first placed with a lady who took him to visit older people in nursing homes and assisted-living centers. That was a perfect fit for Shaq's sweet spirit. He somehow seemed to know these people needed a little extra love and gentleness. Then something happened—we don't know what—and Shaq was given to someone else.

Giving a dog away is actually against Old Friends' rules. Any dog that has to leave its foster home is supposed to be returned to the sanctuary. This is so that Old Friends can

make sure all its dogs stay in homes where they will be loved and safe. But Shaq didn't end up in a loving and safe place. He was given away again and yet again—moving at least three or four times in just a few weeks. Somehow he landed in a rescue shelter in East Tennessee. Thankfully Shaq had a microchip, which allowed the staff there to track him back to Old Friends. They called Old Friends and said, "We've got your dog." A volunteer rushed to Knoxville to rescue their friend.

WHAT ARE MICROCHIPS?

Microchips are a wonderful way to protect lost pets. A tiny computer chip is placed under the animal's skin, usually on the back of its neck. The microchip is very small—about as big as a grain of rice—so it doesn't hurt. When someone finds a lost pet, a vet's office or shelter uses a special scanner to read the information on the chip, which tells who the animal belongs to. They can then contact the owner and get that pet safely home.

When Shaq arrived back at the sanctuary, he was terrified. All the noise of the other dogs was just too much for this gentle soul. He spent his days in the calm and quiet of the vet's office.

Rita was already a volunteer at Old Friends when Shaq

came in. She and her husband, Bill, had just lost their own two dogs—both within just two weeks. Those losses had left a huge, dog-shaped hole in their hearts. Rita and Bill were on the lookout for a new senior friend to love, and they thought Shaq might be just the dog for them. In fact, the first time Bill saw Shaq, he *knew* this dog needed them and they needed him. It took a little time for Shaq to agree with them though.

With all he'd been through, Shaq was afraid of change and new people. Rita and Bill were patient and gave him the time he needed to get to know them. Every day for two weeks, they came to visit Shaq in the vet's office. Eventually Shaq warmed up to them and even allowed Bill to brush him—and that was the beginning of an amazing friendship.

When, at last, it was time to take Shaq home, Bill led him into the house and took off his leash. Shaq wandered around a bit, trying out all the different dog beds they had spread out for him. Then he plopped down in the middle of the carpet and went to sleep—as if he knew he was finally home. Which, of course, he was.

Biscuit Run

Once Shaq settled in, he and Bill quickly came up with their own special tradition. Every Saturday morning, they pile into the car and head to McDonald's. Or Chick-fil-A. Or

Bojangles'. Or wherever their biscuit cravings take them. There, they order the breakfast biscuit specialty of the house. (*Shhh!* Don't tell Shaq, but those biscuits are really a way to get him to take his medicine!) All the drive-through employees know and love Shaq. Then, doggy bags in hand, they head back home for a feast.

Shaq knows when it's time to make a biscuit run. If Bill is running behind, he'll bark to let him know it's time to hit the road! Lately, though, Shaq has taken to barking on mornings other than Saturday. And who can blame him? Doesn't Tuesday sound like a good day for a biscuit run too?

Biscuit time isn't the only time Shaq knows. He also knows when it's playtime. Every afternoon at three o'clock, Shaq will scurry to find a toy and then plop it down at Bill's and Rita's feet. That's because three in the afternoon is playtime, when they all head outside for a lively game of fetch. Don't be late!

THE COWARDLY LION

Do you remember the Cowardly Lion from *The Wizard of Oz*? He looks all big and tough and scary, but he's really a great, big coward. Well, that's Shaq. He looks all big and tough and scary, but he's really a big scaredy-cat . . . *er*, dog, that is.

"If we come home and walk in the back way," Rita says,

"Shaq will hear the noise. He'll come creeping down—like he knows it's his job to protect the house, but you can tell he really doesn't want to. He steps out into the hall, all scared-looking. When he sees it's us, you can see him thinking, *whew*. After that, he'll run over to greet us."

When it's time to go outside, if Shaq spots a strange car in the neighbor's driveway, he'll run out, do his business, and sprint right back in. Poor Shaq even hides from his fast-food friends when they call out to him on his weekly biscuit run. And though Shaq loves to take walks on his favorite greenway, he will refuse to get out of the car if he sees a truck, hears a strange sound, or smells something that makes him uncomfortable. (If he does get out of the car, be prepared to stay awhile though. Shaq wants to stop and smell *everything*!)

While Shaq may not be the king of the forest, he definitely holds a lion-sized spot in Bill's and Rita's hearts.

What Is a Newfoundland?

The Newfoundland, also known as the Newf, can weigh up to 150 pounds! In spite of their huge size, however, they are considered the sweetest dogs. They especially love children. A Newf went with explorers Lewis and Clark on their journey across the North American continent back in the early 1800s.

Mr. Sensitive

While Shaq may look like a beast, he's really very sensitive. In fact, he can easily get his feelings hurt. For example, Shaq hates taking pills, so the vet once tried to hide his medicine in a lump of peanut butter. Shaq just looked at her and walked away, pouting. He seemed to say, *Really? Do you think I'm going to fall for that?*

This big softie is also sensitive to how others feel. When Bill and Rita caught a bad virus, Shaq lay beside them the whole time. And when Bill's mother was in a rehabilitation facility, Shaq went to visit. When he saw her, he immediately put his feet on the bed, climbed up on that little twin-size bed with her, and lay down beside her—and she just loved it.

Who wouldn't?

Sooo Loud!

Shaq may be a big softie, but his bark is impossible to ignore. It's big and loud and just a little bit scary. It almost looks like he's biting the air when he barks. If he really wants something, he'll bark and bark and keep on barking. If you didn't know him, you'd think he was going to tear you up.

Fortunately for Bill and Rita, Shaq didn't really bark the first month or so they knew him. (If he had, they might have been too scared to take him home.) Now they know his big bark is just that—all bark. These days, Shaq talks to them quite a bit . . . and he mostly remembers to use his inside voice.

Shaq's bark isn't the only thing that's loud. He snores . . . *really loud.* "It's just amazing how loud he is," Bill says. Like rattle-the-windows loud. And his snores come with lots of variety. He might start out with a regular old *Snnggg-shew! Snnggg-shew!* Then all of a sudden he'll throw in a *Snort! Snoot! Snuffle! Snnnnnnggg-ggg-ggg!* before settling back into sawing logs.

How do Shaq's humans sleep with all the noise? "We sleep great!" Rita says. "I don't know why, but his snoring is actually very soothing."

When it comes to where Shaq sleeps, he has a few favorite spots—in one of his dog beds, in the hall, or at the end of his humans' bed. But his most favorite spot to snooze is Bill's spot. If Bill gets up off the couch, his chair, or even the bed, Shaq will jump right up and steal his spot!

Shaq might steal a snoozing spot, but he doesn't mind sharing his. In fact, he and Bill enjoy napping together on the extra-big lounge chair out on the sunporch. "He's a body hugger," Rita says. "He'll just get right up next to you. It's the best thing. Sometimes it's hard to get anything done because you just want to lie down and take a nap with him."

COME ON IN, THE WATER'S FINE!

Shaq's forever home is on the lake, and Bill and Rita have discovered that he loves to play in the water. "He must have spent some time on a boat or near water," Bill says, "because he is such a great swimmer." Now Bill and Rita toss balls into the lake for him, and Shaq races right in after them. There's also a nearby beach area where Shaq can go for a swim.

But swimming in a quiet lake is nothing like swimming in the waves of the ocean. When Rita and Bill took their gentle giant to Florida for the first time, they wondered whether he'd be courageous enough to go for a swim. They went to a quiet beach in October, when there weren't many people around to frighten him. It took a little while, but Shaq couldn't resist the water. Each day he got a little braver and a little braver. Finally he would swim out to Bill. "He's just such a beautiful swimmer," Bill says. "He just glides through the water."

One of the last days they were at the beach, a family was out in the ocean playing a game of catch with a football. Shaq lay in the sand watching them—until he just couldn't stand it any longer. He jumped up, gathered his courage, and swam out to them—which was amazing because he's usually terrified of strangers! They even tossed the ball to him. "Shaq wanted that football so bad," Rita says, "so he got one for Christmas!"

STOP THAT SQUIRREL!

If you want to see this gentle giant get really excited, just say, "Hey, Shaq! Where's that squirrel? He's out there! He's getting the birdseed!"

You see, Rita and Bill have a bird feeder right outside of their sunroom. Squirrels love to steal the birdseed. And it tears Shaq up. At the first hint of a thieving squirrel, he'll instantly jump up and run to chase the pest away. He never bothers the birds though. He seems to know that the food is for them.

Another thing that will get Shaq moving is a cat. Even the word *cat* is enough to send him scrambling. All Bill and Rita have to say is "Oh, there's a kitty! *Meow, meow, meow, meow*"—and Shaq is off to find that cat!

PAWSOME FACTS ABOUT SHAQ

Shaq has lots of little quirks, and these odd little things make him even more lovable.

- Fetch is Shaq's favorite game. Rita can sometimes coax him to take a longer walk by tossing a toy out ahead of him.
- If you really want to make Shaq's tail wag, scratching at the base of his tail or behind his ears is just the thing.
- Shaq doesn't like it when Rita and Bill watch basketball or football games because they get too loud and excited.

- Shaq loves to play with his favorite four-legged friends—Dexter and Miss Chewie. These senior dog buddies belong to a friend of the Jakeses. Dexter is a dachshund, and Miss Chewie is a "Doxiepoochi"—a dachshund, poodle, and Chihuahua mix. These three friends even have doggy sleepovers!
- Shaq wants his people to stick together. If they're all out at the greenway together and Shaq gets tired, Bill will start back to get the car. Shaq will go after him and pull Rita along. "He wants us all to be together," Rita says. "It's very sweet."

Just the Right Spot

While it sounds crazy to us, lots of dogs absolutely love scratches on the bum. That's probably because that spot on their back by their tail is just full of nerve endings—and it's one of the few places dogs can't scratch themselves!

Courage Grows in Love

Shaq came to Old Friends shaking and frightened. But little by little, he's letting go of those fears and soaking in the tail-wagging goodness of his new life with Rita and Bill. "I love it when he's confident and not afraid," Rita says. "He'll still get scared sometimes. And we just wish he knew that he never has to be afraid again."

Instead of fear, his days are now filled with biscuit runs, walks in the park, and chasing squirrels—along with lots of love and affection from his favorite people.

"You just say 'Shaq,' and we get happy," Rita says. And just one look at Shaq curled on his favorite chair is all it takes to know that Shaq is indeed happy too.

PRINCE

THE DUDE OF DOGS

Prince is so chill, nothing flusters him. He's the royal Dude of Dogs!

BREED: dachshund

AGE: 14 years old

SIZE: about 14 pounds

GENDER: male

PRINCE'S PEOPLE: Julie and Don Rietdorf

FUN FACT

While most dachshunds like to burrow into blankets, Prince hates to be covered up. If anyone tries to cover him, he'll dig his way out, huffing and *harrumph*ing until he's free.

Meeting Prince Charming

Prince is one of the few dogs whose story is known to Old Friends. He lived a good life in a happy home with a couple who lived not too far from the sanctuary. Then suddenly, the husband passed away. The wife tried to keep Prince, but she worked long hours, and he was left alone most of the time. She knew this was not fair to Prince. She had heard about Old Friends and reached out to them for help. Though Old Friends was not able to take Prince into the sanctuary (they only take dogs from shelters), they reached out to fosters Julie and Don.

The first time Julie and Don met Prince was at a lunch. They had seen his picture and had agreed to foster him until a forever home could be found. But the first time Julie saw Prince, she thought, *He's gorgeous!* And Don said, "Look at all that hair!" (Prince is a long-haired dachshund.) "You'd think with all that hair it would get tangled up, but it doesn't," Julie says. "It's just so soft and silky."

Though the Rietdorfs were only supposed to be temporary fosters, it didn't take ten minutes with Prince for him to find a forever place in their hearts. Julie told Old Friends right then and there at the lunch, "Don't look for anyone else. We're keeping him."

Nothing Stops This Prince

The only thing that made Julie and Don hesitate just a little is the fact that Prince is blind. At that time, they had never had a blind dog. Taking in Prince was a little scary at first because they weren't sure what to expect. They didn't know what Prince would be able to do for himself and what they would need to do for him. As it turns out, Prince is one sharp pooch. Julie and Don were amazed by how quickly he figured everything out in his new home. In fact, he figured it out *so* quickly that they thought maybe he wasn't completely blind.

"Then," Julie says, "we had him out in the yard, and he walked right into a tree. And I thought, *Well, he is blind after all!*" Don't worry though. Prince wasn't hurt. Within just a few hours on that first day, Prince knew how to get to the door to go outside, he knew how to go down the few short steps to the yard, *and* he had already started figuring out the yard—including where all the trees were!

Prince now loves to wander around the yard on his own. Anytime the door is opened, he's right there, ready to go outside. As he gets older, he does tire out a bit more quickly. Instead of waiting until he gets inside to take a nap, he'll just plop down in the grass for a little refreshing snooze.

Because of Prince, Julie and Don now believe that blind dogs are even smarter than seeing dogs. They have since taken in two more blind dogs.

Senior Speed

Julie and Don have always loved and kept dogs. But how did they end up caring for senior dogs? Well, it all started with a beautiful—and *young*—golden retriever.

Julie and Don's daughter is a vet tech, which is like a nurse for animals. She called them one day to tell them about a golden retriever that had come in to be checked before being sent to a rescue. She knew her parents loved goldens, and she said, "You've got to meet this dog!" So Julie and Don went to the vet to meet him.

"This was such a beautiful dog," Julie says. "But he was

about four years old, and he had *so* much energy. If someone hadn't been holding the leash, he would have jumped over the fence! By that time, Don and I were retired, and we looked at each other and said, 'We don't have the energy for this!' Now if we had thought he was in danger of being put down, we would have taken him no matter what. But he was going to a rescue, and we knew he would find a safe home."

Julie and Don had already been following Old Friends on Facebook for a while. On the way home from visiting that golden, they decided maybe it was time to fill out an application.

"Senior dogs are more our speed," Don says. "We didn't really realize that until we met that four-year-old golden. But that's how we got started with senior dogs."

Senior dogs are just right for people without a lot of extra energy or time. They still do all the things puppies do—they love to play, go for walks, and cuddle. They also have wonderful personalities, and as Don says, "They're easier to catch when they run off."

"They just need a chance," Julie says. "And that's what we want to do—give them a chance."

TEN DOGS AND COUNTING

Prince was Julie and Don's second old friend. Both Julie and Don volunteer at the sanctuary, often helping to transport

the dogs to medical appointments. They also pick up dogs from shelters and bring them to Old Friends. Turns out, though, that spending time in a car with a senior friend can be a dangerous thing . . . because you just might end up falling in love with them.

"Soon we had four dogs." Don laughs. "And we said, 'Four is enough.' Then it was 'six is enough.' When we got to eight, we said, 'Eight is enough.' . . . Then we came across a bonded pair, and we said, 'Ten is enough.' But really, ten *is* enough." At least until the next dog needs a lift in their car and they fall in love again.

"We'd love to have a ranch with two hundred acres," Don dreams, "and just fill it up with about thirty dogs and a bunch of horses and other animals. We'd take them all in."

Is it tough keeping up with ten dogs, many of whom are on special diets and medicines? It can certainly be a bit crazy at times, especially mealtimes. But Julie says, laughing, "I was a nurse before I retired, so I'm used to having lots of patients. And these dogs don't talk back and complain like people patients do sometimes. Although when I'm trying to get everyone fed, they can get a little noisy. I just have to remind them that there are ten of you and only one of me!"

And with ten dogs scampering around, it can be a challenge to keep up with them all. "At bedtime or whenever we leave to go somewhere, we do a head count," Don says. "We don't want to accidentally forget anybody or leave anybody outside."

A Dog by Any Other Name

Julie and Don like to give all of their dogs a middle initial—and then they make up all kinds of names to fit the initials. But Prince has *two* initials: Prince E. B., which comes from the way they say his name—"Princey B."

On some days, when Prince is running around and around and going crazy, the E. B. stands for "Energizer Bunny." And on other days, E. B. stands for "Elmo's Brother." (Elmo is one of Prince's fur-brothers.)

Another of Prince's nicknames is "The Dude" because he's so laid back. He also goes by the name of "Mr. Cool." "Nothing bothers him," Don says. "He's like an ice cube. Just very chill."

But no matter what you call him, he's definitely one charming Prince!

A Day in the Life of a Prince

As you might expect, Prince gets the royal treatment. He's up at about seven each morning for a quick trip outside to take care of business. Julie, with her nursing skills, then takes the morning breakfast shift. She makes sure Prince and all the other dogs in his court get their morning kibble and medicines.

After breakfast, it's time for another stroll around the

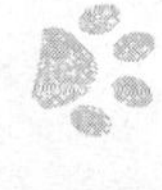
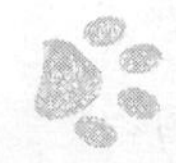

backyard kingdom. And since being royal is exhausting, he might take a nap or two while he's out there. If he happens to step on a squeaky toy in one of his laps around the kingdom, he'll stop to play with it for a bit before moving on to his next napping spot.

A little snack in the afternoon keeps Prince's energy up, so he can make it to his next royal nap. When it's treat time, Prince would like the soft ones, please. And Julie and Don had better make sure he gets his royal dinner feast on time. Prince can get a little "hangry" if they're running behind.

After dinner, there are a couple more naps to take care of. Then it's outside for one last stroll around the backyard to take care of royal business before bed. Prince likes to keep in touch with all of his royal subjects. So bedtime is downstairs with the other dogs. A good, long snooze brings an end to His Highness's day.

BELLY RUBS, BUT NO HUGS

Like many dogs, Prince loves to have his belly rubbed. Don laughs and says, "You know how some dogs will flip over for a belly rub whenever somebody walks close by? Well, I guess since Prince is blind, he doesn't really know when someone is close or not. So every now and then, he'll just flip over for a belly rub."

"I might be on the other side of the room," Julie says,

"and I'll see him flip over for a belly rub. I just laugh and tell him, 'Okay, Prince. I'm coming.'" *Ahhh*, belly rubs on demand. It's good to be royal, isn't it, Prince?

But beware! While Prince loves his belly rubs, he absolutely hates hugs. No crowding of the royal person, please.

WHAT IS A DACHSHUND?

Dachshunds are also called wiener dogs because of their long bodies. They were first bred more than three hundred years ago in Germany to be badger hunters. Their long, slim bodies allowed them to burrow into badger dens. *Dachs* is German for "badger," while *hund* means "dog."

THE PROFESSIONAL NAPPER

Prince is not much of an adventurer. These days, his greatest adventures are all about where to take his next nap. "Prince is always in the mood for a nap," Don says. "He is a professional napper!"

Prince's favorite places to nap are in one of the many dog beds Julie and Don keep scattered around. Or if Julie is busy with the wash, he might climb up on a pile of laundry to keep her company while he sneaks in a little shut-eye.

Anytime the urge to nap hits him, Prince will just stop wherever he happens to be—inside or outside—and curl up for a little catnap . . . *um*, dognap.

A Chance to Shine

Prince may be blind, but he has never let that slow him down or stop him from doing what he wants to do. And he doesn't let it upset him either. Prince keeps a very laid-back attitude, even when life gets "bumpy." Because he's blind, he will sometimes bump into one of the other dogs. (Unlike the walls and furniture, the other dogs tend to move around, of course!) A couple of them will get a little snippy with him. But Prince just seems to say, *Okay, sorry about that. I'll just go another way.*

Prince doesn't let his blindness or his age keep him from searching for all the best that life with Julie and Don has to offer.

The Rietdorfs know that some people worry that having an old friend will be too hard because they won't have the dog for as long. But Julie says, "Instead of thinking about how sad it is or how long we'll have them, I think about how much we improve their lives. And that makes it worthwhile to us. Yes, it is hard sometimes. And if it ever stops being hard, then something is wrong and we need to stop doing it."

It's the harder things in life that are often the best things.

"Old friends need a home," Julie says, "and they need the love we can give them even more than the younger dogs."

"Every dog is amazing in its own kind of way," Don says. "Every dog at Old Friends has its own personality. And every single one is a wonderful, wonderful little creation. They just need a chance to shine."

WALLY

A GOOD DOG

If you ask Sally to pick one of her favorite old friends to talk about, it's quite a struggle to pick just one. That's because Sally has had over twenty-eight old friends come into her home—six of them are still living with her now. But Wally holds an extra-special place in her heart.

BREED: black mixed breed (mutt)

AGE: around 14 years old

SIZE: 45 pounds

GENDER: male

WALLY'S PERSON: Sally McCanner

FUN FACT

Wally has the most *soulful* eyes—as if you can see down into his soul. They are filled with emotion, and you can tell he is thinking deep and important things.

A Friend to Special Old Friends

Sally works at the sanctuary, helping to make sure all the dogs—both in the sanctuary and in the forever foster homes—get all the medicines and medical care they need. With hundreds of dogs under the care of Old Friends, that's a full-time job! And because Sally sees all the dogs who need a little extra love and attention, they are the ones who catch her eye. She has taken in dogs who are blind, deaf, and diabetic. She has taken in dogs who are sick with cancer or who struggle with fear and anxiety. If there's a dog with an extra-special need, then there's a good chance it'll find a home with Sally. As she says, "I take the dogs with issues, and I make sure they have the best life I can give them."

With all those dogs, you can see why it would be almost impossible to pick a favorite. But there is one who is a little extra special to Sally—Wally.

When asked to describe Wally, Sally says, "He's just this really big, black, fuzzy dog. He reminds me of the big, black dog from *Harry Potter*. In fact, I almost changed his name, but then I decided Wally suited him just fine."

WHAT IS A MUTT?

Wally is what is often called a **mutt**. A mutt is a dog who is a mix of two or more different breeds. Mutts are often a combination of all the very best parts and personalities of their purebred ancestors. They come in all shapes and sizes, depending on who their parents are. Mutts, or mixed-breed dogs, are affectionate and faithful to their families and make excellent pets. In other words, a mutt is just a really good dog. Like Wally.

A Special Connection

Sally first met Wally when she was working as a volunteer at the sanctuary. That was in the early days of Old Friends, when they were still at the cabin. Things were getting crowded, and one day at a meeting, Zina asked Sally if she would take Wally home with her. Even though Sally had never even met Wally, she said, "Sure."

Wally went home with Sally after the meeting that very day, and he settled right into her home, as if he'd always belonged there.

"He's just a sweet dog," Sally says. "You can't help but love him. He was about ten years old when I got him, and I've had him for four years now. That makes him probably close to fourteen years old. He's starting to slow down a little in his old age, but he's still pretty healthy. He's just a good old dog.

"It's not that there's anything remarkable about Wally. He doesn't really play with a bunch of toys or anything. He mostly keeps to himself. But Wally and I just have this special connection," Sally says. "He loves me, and I love him."

Mornings with Wally

With so many dogs around, mornings can be a little crazy. Sally gets up and lets everyone outside first. Then there are

all those little mouths to feed. "That's when I'm the belle of the ball," Sally says. "Everyone loves to see me at mealtime!" And because so many of her old friends have health problems, most of them have a different, special food to eat and their own medicines to take. After breakfast, it's time for another trip outside.

Once everyone is settled, that's when it's Wally's special time. Sally grabs her coffee and heads to the recliner for a bit of peace and quiet. Wally always comes over and lies down next to her chair. But before he lies down, he rests his head on her knee. That's Sally's cue to pet him and give him a little extra-special attention. After that, Wally will settle down to nap at her feet. All the other dogs seem to know this is Wally's special time with Sally. And it's a time that both Wally and Sally look forward to every day.

BEFORE OLD FRIENDS

Before Sally began working with old friends, she worked to train puppies as guide dogs for the blind. "I loved working with those puppies because they were all Labs or Lab-and-golden mixes. And I just love their personalities. I would get a puppy when it was about seven to eight weeks old—when it still had that sweet puppy breath. I would work with it until it was twelve to fifteen months old, and then it would go back to the guide dog association for the next stage of its training."

While the puppies were with Sally, they learned to lead people up and down steps, to behave in restaurants, and to walk around downtown. They learned to get used to people and cars and not to get distracted by them. Sally even took some of her puppies to work with her, which the people in her office loved. "In fact," Sally laughs, "if I showed up to work without a puppy, people acted like, 'Why are you here if you don't have a puppy?' "

Sally believes it was working with service dogs for the blind and being around the blind community that drew her to working with old friends who were blind. "Living in that community has given me a deeper affection and understanding for blind dogs," she says.

Extra-Special Old Friends

While many old friends are quite healthy and playful, a few have some extra needs. These are the ones who hold a special place in Sally's heart. She rarely picks out her dogs. Instead, she takes the dogs who need her. And perhaps because of her years spent working with guide dogs for the blind, she is especially fond of the blind dogs.

"They just need boundaries," Sally explains. "They need walls and fences to keep them from getting lost, and they need to have steps blocked off so they don't fall."

Blindness isn't as big of an adjustment for a dog as it is

for a person. That's because sight isn't a dog's main sense. It's much harder for dogs if they lose their sense of smell or hearing because they rely on those senses most. Blind dogs, however, quickly learn how to get where they need to go and do what they need to do.

At Sally's house, there is a large area just for the blind dogs. She gives them their own space so they don't have to worry about bumping into the other dogs and upsetting them. There's even a balcony, fully fenced in, so the dogs can come and go as they please.

KEEP GOING

Most of the dogs who come to live with Sally have to deal with some pretty big struggles, such as blindness, illness, or anxiety. But they keep going. And they keep loving the people who love them.

Whether it's refusing to get upset when they get bumped around or having to wait their turn for breakfast, patience and that "keep going" spirit keep these dogs' tails wagging. And seeing their happiness is what keeps Sally going.

"I keep telling myself," Sally says, "that whatever time they had with me could have been the best time of their lives."

ZELDA

THE QUEEN

Queen Zelda often wears a frosty look on her face, but underneath, her heart is a warm beam of sunshine.

BREED: beagle-hound mix

AGE: 14 years old

SIZE: 35 pounds

GENDER: female

ZELDA'S PERSON: Jenny Cruise

FUN FACT

Jenny calls Zelda "the Queen" because she can be a bit snooty. Whether she's happy or sad, playful or annoyed, Zelda always keeps a cool, queenly expression on her face.

One Lucky Pup

Neither Jenny nor Old Friends know much about Zelda's history. She was turned in to a local animal control center, but no one knows why. Jenny often wonders if Zelda had a good life before she came to her. "She's not afraid or anything," Jenny says, "so I don't think anyone had hurt her. And I try not to judge. You never know what people are going through. There may have been an illness or a loss or an accident, and the family may not have been able to care for Zelda."

Jenny first met Zelda after responding to a plea that Old

Friends put out on the special Facebook page for forever fosters. The sanctuary was full, so Zelda and some other dogs had been staying at a boarding kennel. But it was spring break, and the boarding kennel needed all of its spots for clients. Old Friends was looking for people to take dogs for just a couple weeks, until the dogs could go back to boarding. Jenny had fostered before, so she thought, *Sure. Just give me one. I don't care which one.*

Zelda was the lucky pup.

"She first went to the vet to be checked out," Jenny remembers. "I picked her up there. When I went to put her in the car, I had to put some things in the trunk first. As soon as I popped open the trunk, Zelda jumped right in. That's how excited she was to go." Of course, Jenny then had to talk Zelda into getting out of the trunk and into the car with her.

From the moment Zelda walked into Jenny's house that first day, she acted as if she'd lived there forever. "She didn't hesitate at all. She just walked right in and made herself at home," Jenny says. "It was like, *Okay, this is my new home. This is my roommate.*"

Such a Charmer!

Zelda was only supposed to stay with Jenny for a couple weeks, until spring break was over. Looking back, Jenny laughs. "You can see the timeline on my Facebook page. First I said, 'Hey, everybody! This is Zelda. She's going to be staying with us for a couple of weeks.' One of my friends commented, '*Aaandd* now you have another dog.'" (Jenny already had a basset hound named Lucy and a Jack Russell terrier named Callahan.)

Jenny, of course, said it was only temporary. Then, about five days later, she posted, "This is Zelda's new dog bed. That doesn't mean she's staying here. I just wanted to get her a bed." About five days after that, Jenny bought her a name tag with her address on it. "And that's when I kind of knew she was staying," Jenny says. So she called Old Friends and told them, "I'm gonna hold on to Zelda."

What Is a Beagle?

Beagles are small hunting dogs that have been around for centuries. They have excellent sniffing skills and are often used for hunting rabbits. They are known for their sweet puppy-dog faces, friendly personalities, and "singing" skills.

What made Jenny decide to give Zelda a forever home? "She just charmed me," Jenny says. "She is so sweet and very quiet. She was already house-trained. I'm out all day at work, but she never tears anything up or messes with

anything. Being older, she was already through with all that chewing and stuff. She gets along great with the other dogs. I've never even had to crate her. So I thought, *Why not? Why not keep her?* She's just a sweet, old lady." That was back in 2016, when Zelda was about ten years old. She's been with Jenny ever since.

No Guilt, Just Happiness

Like so many others, Jenny first came across Old Friends on Facebook. That was back in 2014 or so. "I was scrolling through their page and became obsessed with the dogs," Jenny says. "I reached out and put in an application." About two weeks later, Jenny brought home her first old friend, a beautiful little basset hound named Lucy. Soon she was volunteering at Old Friends, and now she serves on the board.

One of the things Jenny loves most about Old Friends is that they try to keep everything positive. They don't dwell on the bad things that happen. They celebrate the dogs and their lives. "I think that's why it's so successful and popular," Jenny says. "There's not any guilt. There's not any tears. Everything is positive and happy." Right down to the handwritten thank-you notes for donations.

Old Friends also invites people to see what's happening in the sanctuary with their webcam feeds and Facebook posts. People get to see and keep up with the dogs. "They get attached to certain dogs," Jenny says. "They want to help."

A Heart of Gold

Not too long ago, Lucy, the basset hound, slipped away after a beautiful and well-loved last few years with Jenny, Callahan, and Queen Zelda. And though Zelda doesn't often seek out attention for herself, she seemed to know that Jenny needed a bit of extra comforting. Usually if anyone sits down next to Zelda on the couch, she'll hop off and be on her way—don't crowd Her Highness, please! But after the loss of Lucy, Zelda would come up to Jenny and lick her face as if to say, *It'll be okay. I'm here for you.*

And when Callahan (who hates riding in the car) has to go for a ride, Zelda will lay her head on him to comfort him. There's a heart of gold under that queenly crown!

The Queen and the Clown

Zelda may be the queen, but Callahan is definitely more of a clown. He's a big and lovable Jack Russell terrier who's just a bit wild. Zelda gets along with him pretty well for the most part. Though she prefers to have the couch all to herself, she will share it with Callahan—once in a while. *Occasionally.* Okay, Zelda hardly ever shares the couch with Callahan, but it has happened at least once. Jenny has proof on her camera.

An interesting (and icky) thing Callahan loves to do is lick the inside of Zelda's ear. It's crazy! Zelda won't share a couch with Callahan, but if he wants to lick her ear? Well, that's okay. According to the vet, there's just something about the taste of earwax that some dogs love. (Yes, Jenny checked, because it's weird and gross.)

Hmm, maybe you'll find earwax flavor on your next trip down the dog-food aisle.

WHERE'S ZELDA?

Zelda is a hider. Sometimes Jenny will come home from work, and Her Majesty the Queen is nowhere to be found. Once Jenny searched the whole house—more than once—calling her name and opening every door and looking in every room. At last she found Zelda in the spare bedroom, curled up behind a big pillow, sound asleep.

There are times when Jenny wonders if Zelda is losing her hearing. Or if she's just exercising her royal right to ignore her subjects while catching up on her beauty sleep.

The Tomboy Queen

While Zelda may rule the inside of the house with queenly grace, outside is another story. Queen Zelda transforms into a royal tomboy. Her most favorite thing to do? Dig for moles in the yard. She has single-handedly taken out quite a few of the little kingdom invaders. Sometimes Callahan will steal one and try to pretend he was the one who hunted down the pest, but Jenny knows better. Zelda is queen hunter in this backyard!

If she can get into the backyard, that is.

"I hate to say this about my sweet Zelda," Jenny laughs, "but she's a bit goofy. And maybe not quite so smart. For example, sometimes I'll open the sliding glass door to let her outside. Of course, with sliding glass doors, one side opens and one side doesn't. She will stand by the side that doesn't open and bark like she's trapped. I have to lead her over to the other side. Sometimes Zelda's just not the brightest bulb, but I love her."

Once she figures out the whole sliding glass door thing though, Zelda appreciates the finer things that the outdoors has to offer—like a good roll in the mud. Which, of course, then means it's bath time.

Except Zelda hates baths. *Hates baths*. Jenny laughs. "You'd think that after all this time and all these baths, she would figure out that she is going to live through it. But every time, she acts like she's going to die. I try to comfort her by singing to her, which might actually make it worse because I'm a terrible singer. She will look at me like, *Would you just hush? And plus, I'm, like, deaf!"*

After a bath, Zelda makes sure Jenny knows she is royally angry. As soon as she can, Zelda sneaks away to the nearest patch of dirt or mud to get rid of that disgusting clean, soapy smell. Ahh, the sweet smell of dirt. Maybe with a touch of mole to freshen it up.

Oh, Zelda.

Pawsome Facts About Zelda

- The couch is Zelda's favorite place for napping . . . at least as long as she can have it all to herself. Try to join her, and she'll probably hop down to find another spot. For bedtime she likes to be in the same room as Jenny—not too close, just in the same room. A bed on the floor will do just fine, thank you.
- Who does Zelda think is the coolest guy ever? Chris, the pest control man! He only comes around once every three months, but whenever she sees him, Zelda goes crazy. Maybe it has something to do with those dog treats he keeps in his pocket.
- The tastiest treat ever, Zelda will tell you, is a rubber Kong toy stuffed with little treats and capped off with frozen

peanut butter. She loves figuring out how to get all the treats out of the Kong and into her tummy.

- Zelda loves to be petted on her head. Well, actually, Jenny isn't completely sure. Maybe Zelda just allows Jenny to pet her head in order to make Jenny happy. Chances are, Zelda does like it though . . . after all, a nice scalp massage probably feels pretty good after wearing your crown all day.

A Queenly Gift

There's no way of knowing what kind of life Zelda had in the past. It might have been wonderful or terrible. Jenny knows there's nothing she can do to change any of that. What she *can* do is make a difference in Zelda's life today and in all the days to come. Peanut butter–stuffed Kongs, a backyard to roll in, and a comfy throne are just the beginning. It's Jenny's gifts of love and time and attention that make the real difference—and Zelda gives those gifts right back to Jenny a thousand times over.

MACK

AMERICA'S BEST FRIEND

Mack is a celebrity—and not just at Old Friends. Thanks to his social media fame, people travel from all over the world to meet this floppy-eared, shaggy-furred guy.

BREED: cocker spaniel

AGE: between 10 and 14 years old

SIZE: about 22 pounds

GENDER: male

MACK'S PEOPLE: Mason and Nell Taylor

FUN FACT

Mack is a climber. If he can get his paws on it—a chair, a sofa, your lap—he's going to be climbing up.

What's Up with Those Crazy Bangs?

One of the first things you might notice about Mack is his haircut. Mack wears his bangs combed down over his eyes. Now you might wonder, *How does he see through all that hair?* Well, he doesn't. Mack is blind.

When Mack was first rescued from a local shelter back in 2016, he had severe **glaucoma** in both eyes. Glaucoma (*glaw-KOH-muh*) is an extremely painful eye disease. It not only causes trouble with a dog's ability to see, but it also can give a dog terrible headaches. A dog suffering from glaucoma often won't feel like playing or even eating. The veterinarian decided the best treatment for Mack was to remove his eyes. While that sounds terrible to us, for Mack, it was the beginning of a whole new life.

Dogs adapt pretty easily to losing their sight. Basically, as long as blind dogs have walls and doors—and they aren't out in some huge, open space—they can figure it out. They learn how to navigate the space, and they are able to remember it. And Mack has certainly figured out how to make his way around Old Friends. He knows the building—and even the big yard with all its paths and trails—by heart.

After Mack's surgery, he was free of pain at last. He got his spark back and was transformed into a playful pup again! It was that playfulness that was the start of an amazing friendship between Mack and his favorite human, Mason.

It All Started with Tug-of-War

Mason first heard about Mack from his wife, Nell, who began working at Old Friends in early 2019. "She kept telling me about this dog," Mason says. "They grow his bangs out to cover his 'no eyes.'"

A little while later, Mason met Mack on a tour of Old Friends. But it wasn't until Mason actually started working at the dog sanctuary that the two really hit it off. At that time, Mason took care of the building and the grounds, and he started just hanging out with Mack. Then one day, Mason was out back when Mack reached up and grabbed a rag out of his back pocket. That started a lively game of tug-of-war, which was followed by a nice walk outside. "And that," Mason says, "was all she wrote."

Tug-of-war became a daily treat for the two friends. Mack followed Mason everywhere he went at the sanctuary. So when Mason changed jobs at Old Friends and began working in the front office area, it was only natural for Mack to move up too. Each day, as soon as Mason stepped inside Old Friends, Mack's nose started working and he would race to find his pal.

You might say that Mack is now a little spoiled. Actually, you could call him *a lot* spoiled, but no one is complaining, especially not Mack. He spends a good bit of his day on Mason's lap—who has become an expert at working around his four-legged friend.

For a long time, Mack lived at the sanctuary. Because of his anxiety and fear of change, it was where he was happiest. But being around Mason and Nell all day, most every day, for a few months gave Mack a new sense of adventure and courage. So Mason and Nell decided to welcome Mack into their home. At last he has a forever foster home of his very own.

But how does Mason get any work done at Old Friends without Mack on his lap? Don't worry . . . Mack heads into the office every day with Mason and Nell to make sure they stay on top of things. Some days Mack will eat breakfast at home first, and on other days he joins his old friends for a morning meal. Then it's time to get down to business—at least for Mason and Nell. For Mack, it's time to polish up on his professional napping skills. In Mason's lap, of course.

At the end of a "ruff" day, Mack loves to stroll around the yard in his new home or just hang out with his favorite people. In the past, Mack struggled to sleep at night. (Since he is blind, he can't tell when it's dark or light.) Thankfully Mason and Nell have figured out that he sleeps much better if he's under the covers—all the way under the covers! On weekends Mack enjoys being with his people and goes most everywhere they go. And if Mason and Nell ever have to go somewhere that doesn't allow dogs, Mack pops back over to Old Friends for a visit. With Mason and Nell, it's the best of both worlds for Mack—and the perfect happily ever after.

The Adoring Fans

Mack not only has fans from around the world, but those fans actually come to see him at the sanctuary. Some of them come from as far away as Australia! As you might guess, it can be tough to meet lots of new people when you're blind. So how does Mack handle all the attention?

"On tours," Mason explains, "everyone wants to see Mack. As long as someone he knows stays with him, as long as he can smell them, he's okay. He'll do his thing with the

fans for a couple of minutes and then make his way back to where I'm sitting."

Ah, the life of a celebrity!

MACK FOR THE WIN

If you happened to be watching Dog Bowl III in February 2020, you might have spotted Mack. He was one of sixty-five dogs from thirty-two different shelters who were invited to compete.

While Puppy Bowl has been a fan favorite since 2005, Dog Bowl didn't get its start until 2018. Unlike Puppy Bowl, Dog Bowl features dogs ages three to fourteen. The dogs are divided into two teams: Team Goldies and Team Oldies. The dogs then compete on a miniature football field to see who will take home the Super Senior Award. Mack was a superstar for Team Oldies, and he pulled off an amazing performance both on and off the field.

When Mack first received his invitation to Dog Bowl, it was decided that he and Mason would make a big trip out of it. Of course, it's a long way from Mt. Juliet, Tennessee, to New York City, where they hold the Dog Bowl. It would only make sense to fly, right? Well, that's where Mack and Mason ran into a problem. You see, Mack was too big to ride in the plane's cabin with Mason. He would have to travel in a crate that would be packed away in the bottom of

the plane with the golf clubs and skis. (Yikes! Who wants to do that?) The solution? A super-long ride in the car—all the way to New York City.

After all, what dog doesn't love riding in a car? Well, that's when they discovered problem number two. Mack didn't like to ride in cars. At least not at first. Just imagine: You can't see, but you can tell you're moving—*fast.* And there are all these strange sounds and smells coming at you. It's easy to see why Mack would be frightened in the car.

Fortunately for Mack, Mason was patient. At first they just sat in the car. Then, for about a week, they drove around the parking lot. After that, they made it all the way to the local hardware store, where dogs are welcome to walk around. Over the next few days, they kept going for rides. And then three weeks later, they were on their way—all the way to New York City.

And now? Mack's new favorite thing is riding in the car. He absolutely *loves* it. All it takes is hearing the *click* of a leash, and he's ready to go for a ride.

MACK IN THE BIG APPLE

In between filming for the Dog Bowl at Madison Square Garden, Mack toured New York City—also known as the Big Apple. With so many exciting smells and sounds to explore, Mack spent hours and hours walking around the city. Together, Mack and Mason walked a total of fifteen miles in just a day and a half! One of the most amazing things was how many people recognized this celebrity pooch from his social media fame.

So you might be wondering: *In all their wanderings around the city, did Mack sample any of that world-famous New York pizza?* Both he and Mason refused to comment. "There's no proof," Mason states. "Absolutely no proof." Spoken like a politician.

And speaking of politics . . .

Mack for President

In 2019 Mack threw his leash into the race to be president of the United States. In the primary election, Facebook fans voted for their favorite Old Friends pooch. Beating out four other dogs, Mack won by a landslide and was named the official 2020 candidate for the Geezer Party. Of course, this is all just for fun, but doesn't every house need a dog . . . even the White House?

If elected president, Mack promises to be a leader who is always ready to dive in—paws first—and take on the fat cats in Washington. When asked what he would do if those cats were ever to win the majority in Congress, Mack answered:

> First, that would never happen. In the unlikely occasion that it does take place, I will work with the cats to never

put their litter box in a public room; they will have a designated place outdoors. Also, no chasing and pranks in public meetings. I will work hard to gain their trust. "Keep your friends close, and your enemies closer."

Mack stands ready to sniff out any problems and promises to listen to the wishes of voters, especially if they have anything to do with naps or treats. Mack's platform of wisdom, determination, and loyalty are traits that America needs now more than ever.

Politics have definitely gone to the dogs—and with Mack, that's a good thing!

MACK'S OPPONENTS FOR THE GEEZER PARTY NOMINATION

BABS THE BASSET HOUND: Sniffing for Change
FRANCIS THE COONHOUND: Treeing America's Problems
SHARKY THE DACHSHUND: In It for the Long Haul
CHANEL THE CHOW MIX: Put a Queen in the White House

ON THE CAMPAIGN TRAIL

As part of his campaign for president, Mack took time away from his Dog Bowl duties to stop by the White House.

Dressed in his best tuxedo, he posed for a few publicity photos while checking out his possible future workplace. Then it was on to Gettysburg to address the nationwide problem of treat economics. *More treats for all!* Mack says.

Tail-Wagging Role Model

When asked to describe Mack, Mason chooses two words: *determined* and *persistent*. Then he quickly adds a third: *overcomer.*

No one knows exactly what Mack's full history is, but we can guess that it wasn't the best. On top of that, he's had to overcome blindness and anxiety. But in spite of these troubles, he can still show that special kind of love that only a dog can give.

"Look," Mason says, "Mack has had some curveballs thrown at him, but he's hit every one of them out of the park. He's done it with a smile. He's done it with joy. He's done it with love. He's done it with peace. He hasn't taken it on with anger or fighting or a bad attitude. He's taken on all of these challenges in the right way. It's weird to say I'm looking up to a dog, but you know, I am."

With all of his problems and with whatever happened in his past, Mack is always happy and always reaching out to people to make friends. He never gives up.

We can learn a lot from senior dogs like Mack. They

each have a unique story, just like every one of us has a unique story. They all have things to overcome, just like we all have things to overcome. The important thing is to figure out what really matters, things like true friendship.

It's like Mason says when he talks about Mack's approach to life: "Roll with the punches. Bob and weave at whatever comes at you. And things will work out."

In other words, be like Mack.

RECIPES FOR OLD FRIENDS

This recipe makes a food that looks a lot like canned pumpkin or canned dog food, and it's so good for your pup. It's a great place to hide medicines, and the Old Friends gang just loves it! Each dog gets a big spoonful on top of their kibble.

INGREDIENTS

(These amounts don't have to be exact.)
2 pounds boneless chicken breasts and thighs
1 pound whiting fish or catfish
1/4 pound chicken livers and/or gizzards
1/2 pound carrots
1 (12-ounce) box frozen green beans
1/2 cup canned pumpkin
1 apple
1 small sweet potato, cut into large chunks
1/2 cup plain yogurt
1/2 cup psyllium fiber (with no artificial sweeteners)
a heaping tablespoon of coconut oil
1 tablespoon turmeric

STEPS

1. Add the chicken, fish, livers or gizzards, carrots, beans, pumpkin, apple, and sweet potato to a Crock-Pot and cook on low for 12 hours or more. Spoon into a blender or food processor, and blend until smooth. (You may have to do this in batches.)
2. Place in a large bowl.
3. Then add yogurt, psyllium fiber, coconut oil, and turmeric. Mix well.

Use within 4 to 5 days. It can also be frozen.

Dried Sweet Potato Chews

Dogs love these sweet and chewy treats.

INGREDIENTS

2–3 large sweet potatoes, washed thoroughly and dried

STEPS

1. Preheat the oven to 250° F. Line two baking sheets with parchment paper.
2. With a grown-up's help, cut a thin piece of the sweet potato off one of the long edges. (This will help it lie flat while you cut it into slices.)
3. Slice the rest of the potato into thin "chips" that are at least ¼-inch thick. Spread the potato slices on the baking sheets.
4. Bake for 90 minutes. Turn the pieces over and bake for 90 more minutes. This will give you a soft, chewy treat. If your dog likes crunchier chews, bake for 20–30 minutes more. (When you first take the potatoes out of the oven, they may still seem soft. They will dry and harden as they cool.)

Store in the refrigerator for up to 3 weeks, or freeze.

Chicken Soup Cookies

INGREDIENTS

1 cup ground dry dog food kibble

2 cups baking mix

1 (18.8-ounce) can chunky chicken soup

STEPS

1. Preheat the oven to 350° F.
2. Grind kibble in a food processor or blender until it looks like a coarse flour. Grind enough kibble to get 1 cup of "kibble flour."
3. Stir the ground kibble, baking mix, and soup together until well mixed. Drop by teaspoonfuls onto greased cookie sheets. Bake for 15 minutes or until golden brown.

Store in an airtight container in the refrigerator. Makes about 50 to 60 bite-sized treats.

Frosty Treats

INGREDIENTS

32 ounces vanilla yogurt

1 large mashed banana

2 tablespoons peanut butter

2 tablespoons honey

STEPS

1. Add all ingredients to a blender or food processor. Blend until smooth.
2. Pour into an ice cube tray and freeze.

Serve frozen, or let them soften for 10 minutes.

GLOSSARY

alpha: a dominant dog who wants to be the leader of the pack; an alpha dog can be either male or female

blep: when an animal's tongue just barely pokes out of its mouth

bonded pair: two (or sometimes three) dogs who are strongly attached to one another

boof: a low, almost whispered bark

boop: to playfully tap a dog's nose

bork: another word for bark

derp: when an animal's tongue hangs out of its mouth

dock: to shorten a dog's tail; docking may be done for appearance and is common on some dog breeds, or a tail may be docked because of injury

euthanize: a quick and painless method of killing an animal. It's often done by using a shot of medicine that stops the dog's brain, heart, and lungs from working. This is sometimes called being "put to sleep" and is used by some shelters because they have too many dogs to take care of.

forever foster: a person or family who welcomes a pet into their home but does not legally own the pet

glaucoma: an extremely painful eye disease that can cause blindness

hoarding: a situation in which someone has so many animals that the person can't take care of them

isolation: to be separated from other dogs; to be alone

mange: a skin disease in mammals; mange causes itchy and painful sores on the skin

mutt: a dog who is a mix of two or more different breeds

puppy mill: a facility or a person that breeds dogs under terrible conditions in order to get large numbers of puppies to sell

quarantine: to be isolated or separated from others in order to keep diseases from spreading

resource guarder: a dog that is fiercely protective of its things, including food, bowls, toys, and blankets

sanctuary: a safe place; often used to describe a place that rescues and takes care of animals

sedate: to give a drug to make a person or an animal sleep

snoot: a dog's nose

sploot: a position in which a dog stretches out on its tummy with its front paws forward and its legs spread out behind; a sploot is a sign of trust and happiness

veterinarian: a doctor for animals; often called a vet

RESOURCES

Old Friends Senior Dog Sanctuary is a foster-based sanctuary in Mt. Juliet, Tennessee. Visit them online to keep up with all the fun, view dogs waiting for foster homes, browse photos, and even watch the dogs live on the webcam.

website: www.OFSDS.org
Facebook: @OldFriendsSeniorDogSanctuary
Instagram: @ofsds
Live webcam: https://explore.org/livecams/old-friends-senior-dog-sanctuary/senior-dog-gathering-room

If your family is thinking about adopting a pet, check out these adoption tips from the American Society for the Prevention of Cruelty to Animals (ASPCA).

www.aspca.org/adopt-pet/adoption-tips

Leo, Pooh Bear, and other old friends are the stars of the documentary *Seniors: A Dogumentary*. View the trailer, go behind the scenes, and find places to watch the film.

www.SeniorsDogumentary.com

Find a pet to adopt at the Shelter Pet Project, a collaboration between the Humane Society and Maddie's Fund.

www.theshelterpetproject.org/

Visit the American Kennel Club for information on dog breeds, for advice on dog ownership, and to find dog shows near you.

www.akc.org

The Pet Health Network provides articles on pet life stages, nutrition, illness, behavior, and more.

www.pethealthnetwork.com/

Learn about breeds, how to give your pet the best care, how to tell if your pet is sick, and more at Pet MD.

www.petmd.com

Meet all the players in the 2020 Dog Bowl, including Mack.
https://people.com/pets/animal-planet-dog-bowl-2020-adoptable-dogs/